Millie Adams has always loved books. She considers herself a mix of Anne Shirley—loquacious, but charming, and willing to break a slate over a boy's head if need be—and Charlotte Doyle—a lady at heart, but with the spirit to become a mutineer should the occasion arise. Millie lives in a small house on the edge of the woods, which she finds allows her to escape in the way she loves best: in the pages of a book. She loves intense alpha heroes and the women who dare to go toe-to-toe with them...or break a slate over their heads!

Also by Millie Adams

Scandalous Society Brides miniseries

Claimed for the Highlander's Revenge
Marriage Deal with the Devilish Duke
The Duke's Forbidden Ward

Society's Most Scandalous collection

How to Cheat the Marriage Mart

Discover more at millsandboon.co.uk.

THE GOVERNESS AND THE BROODING DUKE

Millie Adams

MILLS & BOON

First published in Great Britain 2023
by Mills & Boon, an imprint of HarperCollins*Publishers* Ltd,
1 London Bridge Street, London, SE1 9GF

www.harpercollins.co.uk

HarperCollins*Publishers*, Macken House, 39/40 Mayor Street Upper,
Dublin 1, D01 C9W8, Ireland

ISBN: 978-0-263-30522-7

06/23

To everyone who needs it.

You are not defined by what hurt you.

And you are worthy of love.

Chapter One

London, 1825

One could never be prepared for a duke.

That was Miss Mary Smith's most prominent thought as she looked up—the natural level of her gaze falling to his black cravat, so great was his height—into the shocking blue eyes of Samuel Montgomery, the Duke of Westmere.

Dressed in a severe black suit which conformed to a body that would look more suited to a Highland warrior than English nobility, he cut an imposing figure.

He was dressed in all black out of concession for mourning, she supposed, and yet it also seemed to suit him.

It was not simply that he was handsome—though he was, and if Mary were the sort of woman who was affected by the handsomeness of men, she would be struck into silence now—it was the vitality and power which shone from him as if he were the sun.

It was unusual to meet the master of the house, as she was accustomed to meeting their wives. Or even a housekeeper.

She understood why she was meeting the Duke himself, though, considering his situation.

She knew little about him, or his situation, apart from the fact he had two children—a boy and a girl—and an infant, who was in the care of a wet nurse since the death of his wife.

The children were young, and without a mother. The potential for the position to go on for years, to allow her some stability, some rest, was high. Higher than either of her previous two positions, where the children had been older when she'd arrived, and nearly finished with the age when a governess was necessary.

Then there was the splendour of the estate. Attingham was glorious, set near the edge of a forest, with spacious lawns all around the red brick and grey stone house. It was, without a doubt, the most beautiful thing she had ever seen, apart from royal residences, in London.

This felt something like hope. For the girl she'd been. That this chance she'd taken, leaving everything behind, coming to England, battling her accent away, and pushing her memories to the side, had all been worth it.

Miss Mary Smith was everything Mary McLaren

had never been. She was calm, assertive and educated. In all things. From arithmetic to society's intricacies.

She prided herself on being unflappable. Unbreakable.

Here and now, when this composure was more important than ever before, she felt herself crack.

She had never met a duke.

Thus was unprepared for the impact of him. Though she did not think one duke was the same as another. Or at least, she had her doubts any were like him.

He was tall, broad-shouldered, his bearing and authority unparalleled to anyone she'd yet met. She had been looked down on before—in both the literal sense and in the figurative. She was quite small, after all.

What the Duke did now was not look *down* on her.

Rather he seemed to look *into* her.

She found she would have preferred a condescending sneer. That, at least, she knew how to withstand.

There were men who sneered because she was a woman, and therefore beneath them. There were women and men who sneered because she was a governess. Not quite a servant. Not quite a lady. Never one of them. A woman who shaped her life around the children of her betters but had none of her own. No husband. Nothing to inherit. Nothing at all to give her value in the way those sorts of people could measure it.

And there were men who sneered in triumph, because they found the arrangement of her features beautiful, and thought because she was a woman, because she was a governess, they could have her if they wished.

The Duke of Westmere did not sneer.

His assessment, clear and cold, was somehow so much more disconcerting for the condescension it lacked.

Despite years of preparing for this very moment, she found there was no way she could have been truly prepared for it. Every moment in England up until this point had been just not quite this.

A meeting with the master's wife was *not quite* a meeting with the master himself. An earl was *not quite* a duke, and his home was *not quite* a duke's home. The lofty air of a man who knew many other men outranked him was not *at all* the bearing of a man who knew that no matter which room he walked into—save one at the palace—none were above him.

Even if this man were to walk into a palace he would stand head and shoulders above anyone else there, she was certain.

She could think of nothing that might lessen his impact.

She might not have been prepared for him specifically, but she was more than prepared for moments where she was out of her depth.

Where she had to crane her neck as if trying to

keep her head above imaginary waves, to keep herself from drowning.

This was what she did now.

She did not look around the stately, well-appointed library, she did not look down at her feet. She met those blue eyes, even though she was terrified to do so. And she smiled.

'It is lovely to make your acquaintance, Your Grace. I have not read the letter the Earl sent you, so if there is anything in that letter you found lacking I shall be happy to supply the information needed.'

He frowned. The corners of his mouth only turned down just slightly, and yet it was as if the temperature of the room had changed.

'You're not English.'

Angst speared her like an arrow, or perhaps it was not her own angst, but that frank, assessing gaze of his.

She had not been wrong.

He *did* see into her.

She was prepared for much, a woman in her position had to be. But she was not prepared for that.

No one outside of boarding school had ever questioned her origins. Not *anyone*. Her accent was good enough to fool the two employers she'd had, and any person she'd had casual acquaintance with. If anyone were to think there was something wrong about her accent, they might think she was simply a girl from

Cheapside trying to sound above herself. But no one had ever suggested she wasn't English.

Her story was easy. Concrete and well-practised. The child of a merchant who had befriended a duke, and upon his death, his child had earned the patronage of the Duke's family.

A lie. A story stolen from the Duke of Kendal's wife, but with permission. Because of her connections to the Laird of her clan, who had paid for her new life in England, Kendal had agreed to act as her patron in England. She had met the man only twice, and his wife four times. But she had been given their explicit instruction to use this story to give herself legitimacy, and so she did.

Yet here that story crumbled, beneath the stark blue gaze of the Duke of Westmere. She knew she could not lie to this man. Not outright.

In which case she had to hope that he didn't ask the right questions. She had to hope she could bend around his sharp pointed questions and supply answers that were close enough. She also had to hope he didn't score any direct blows she couldn't recover from.

You could not bend around a sword if it had run you through.

'No, Your Grace, I am not.'

'*Miss Smith.*' It was a question, but a demand for

information. A wealth of disbelief and condescension in those two simple words she'd chosen as her name.

Mary Smith might understand propriety, she also didn't possess the ability to shrink. She was not a fearful girl any more, and she would not be cowed now. She had lived through too much horror to find the inspection of the peerage to be an assault.

Her secret to making her way through life was that she did not elevate people in her heart. Yes, she knew the rules of society. She observed them. She was practical in all things.

But she believed no man to be better than her, regardless of his title.

She did not shrink beneath the gaze of a man simply because he was male and had been born into an advantageous position.

'A name that was given to me when I came to England to be educated. My benefactor is the former Lady Penelope Hastings, whom I met after she came to Scotland.'

'I know the name.'

'The Duke of Kendal took part in overseeing my safety in England.' This was the truth.

'Well connected.' This was not said with admiration.

She did not require his admiration.

'I am fortunate. There were not many opportunities for me in Scotland, and yet here the world has opened to me.'

She did not tell him she was from what had been a decimated clan in the Highlands, restored by Lachlan Bain upon his return from war with an English bride. Or that Penny had taken an interest in her, not because she was smart, but because she had been sad.

A young girl, pregnant by force at thirteen. The emblem of all that had gone wrong in Clan McKenzie, an affront Lachlan had taken personally.

He had avenged her. Thoroughly. Even though the man had been his own blood.

Perhaps especially because the man was his own blood.

And Mary had been a girl with no education, no husband and no hope of ever rising above what had happened to her, not in that place where everyone had known.

Penny had taken the child—her son—to raise as her own.

She'd had choices.

She could have kept the child. She could have given him to the loving couple who led her clan and give him a position of respect and dignity. It had been no choice. She'd given him a better life.

She could have also stayed and worked in the castle. Watched her son grow up from afar.

But she'd wanted the escape Penny had offered

instead. A new life. One where she didn't have to be Mary McLaren, who had been pinned down in a muddy field behind a grim hut and stripped of her ability to dream that the world might be softer, prettier, better than she'd seen.

She'd wanted her hope back.

England had been a new world when she'd needed it desperately.

She wasn't ashamed to have to admit she wasn't English.

But she was angry to be reminded.

Most days she was Miss Smith with no effort or thought. Once, she'd put her on each day with her chemise, and took her off at the end of the day. Now, even when her skin was bare, she remained Miss Smith.

She resented having to think of sad Mary McLaren.

But she would not let him know that.

'Your former employer had nothing but high praise for you, but I cannot tolerate a liar.' He turned away from her and began to move back to his desk, effectively dismissing her with his posture.

She did know that the proper thing would be to respond to the dismissal. He was a duke. But while she had learned the rules of society, she was not an English miss. He already knew that. And if she did not fight for herself now, she would leave with nothing.

No position, and nowhere to go.

She had nothing to lose now.

'I do not consider myself a liar,' she said. 'Rather I am conscious of the fact that no English parent wants their children to learn to speak with a brogue. I altered my speech in order to better suit my position.'

He did not turn.

'If I may be as honest with you as you have been with me,' she projected her voice a bit too hard. A bit too firm. 'Your Grace,' she added. 'If I were a charlatan this would not be the method by which I made my way in the world. I am a governess because I wish to work, and I wish for that work to matter. I must keep to my own moral code. If I wished to steal from a wealthy man, why would I not make myself his mistress?'

That earned her a response. He turned, just to the side, giving her a view of his profile, his square jaw and strong chin. His shoulders going taut, his body straightening.

'I am not vain,' she continued, 'nor am I unaware of the charms which I possess. If my honour did not matter, if my integrity meant nothing to me, why should I work? For there are more effective ways to disarm a man, are there not?'

One dark brow lifted, just slightly. 'You speak as if you are knowledgeable of the subject.'

Yet again, she felt as if his gaze was the cut of a broadsword.

The *subject*.

What she knew was that men were base. If a woman married a man her body was his. If a woman was on the wrong street and encountered the wrong man, her body was his. Smart women, Mary thought, made their bodies a commodity and forced men to pay for the privilege.

She saw no shame in that. The world demanded women debase themselves for survival. Mary would not judge anyone for how they survived.

A life as a wife. A life in the church. A life as a harlot.

A life as a servant.

In any case, a life lived in supplication to a man.

Yes, she knew of *the subject*.

'I speak as a woman in the world,' she said. 'Not a lady, but one who has had to answer these sorts of difficult questions. How I am to survive? How I am to make my way? I wished to be educated and felt my success would best be found in England. Forgive me again, Your Grace, but if my desire were to fool a man why ever would I take a position with his children, where I am least likely to ever see him?'

He turned to her fully. 'You speak as though you do not hold men in the highest of regards.'

'I do not have to, the entirety of the world does it for me.'

She was on the verge of being thrown out of the room, there was no reason for her to hold her tongue.

If he wished to have honesty she could give him a sliver of her truth, and even that, she had the feeling would be too much for a duke.

He would send her away directly, she had no doubt. She was nearly certain he would do so anyway. It was why she was letting herself speak so freely now.

The truth was, her position as governess allowed her to avoid speaking to men almost entirely. She preferred it that way. She did not allow men to look down their nose at her. And she would not allow this one to do so, even if he were a duke. This, she understood was part of the problem with her not being English. She did not have an innate respect or understanding of the power structure here. She had learned it, she participated in it, she was beholden to it, as was everyone here. But she could not bring herself to be filled with natural awe.

She had lost him, and she could feel that. She also knew that the next moments would betray what manner of man he was. She waited. Looked for that particular glint in his eyes. The one that would betray whether or not he was anticipating her begging for the position. For his good graces. In which case she would see herself out. She refused to work for a man who took joy in the degradation of others. Who took joy in the degradation of women.

There was a difference between being a man of lofty position, who enjoyed the power that came with it as a passive side-effect of the position. And a man who enjoyed it because it meant others were beneath him and had to beg for that which they might receive.

There was a sort of man who was always mindful of which person in the vicinity they might overpower. Whether it be by rank or brute strength.

The truth was, whether the man was a duke or a peasant, the answer was always *a woman*. No matter who else he might have dominion over, physically, any man, regardless of wealth or status could have it over any woman. She was always aware of that. And it was why she always watched a man's eyes. To see what manner of predator she was dealing with.

All men had the capability. But not all men relished this fact.

The Duke's eyes were cool. It was nearly impossible to discern what he might be thinking. Whether he was contemplating throwing her out, offering her a job, or...

She would not give shape or voice to the other thought hovering around the edges of her mind.

She waited. Waited for him to tell her to leave.

'I do not require that you hold me in high regard, Miss Smith,' he said. 'But I do require a qualified governess. One who will treat my children properly and see to their education. Is everything in this letter in regard to your education factual?'

That shocked her, but not enough to silence her.

'Yes. The only thing not present in that letter is my background before I came to England. I was not educated prior to my arrival here. But I have since made up for that. I was in the top of my class at school. I speak French as well as German.'

'And you are quite an accomplished mimic when it comes to accents.'

'I thank you for your notice. Though not accomplished enough that you did not perceive something amiss.'

'Don't take it to heart. I have a reputation for being impossible to lie to.' He looked away for a moment, and then back at her. 'I do not care if you're from Scotland, and you make a good argument for why your particular lies—deception, I should say—aren't relevant to the current situation. Were I in a position to delay finding a governess I would send you away simply on principle. I hope you understand.'

She didn't respond to that, because her only response was tart. And she felt she had likely rather overextended herself in that regard.

His lips curved. Just slightly. As if he had correctly interpreted her silence.

And as his lips curved, it was as if he touched her. Featherlight. In that same curved, sweeping motion and her breath was lost to her.

Was this simply the innate power of a duke?

It couldn't be anything else. Not for her.

'You have my warning. My children are…difficult. They are still coping with the loss of their mother.'

For the first time, she allowed herself to think about that loss in a way that wasn't simply connected to the position she was taking.

'I'm very sorry.' Her mouth had gone quite dry. 'How long has it been?'

'Just near four months. I have been through four governesses in that time. We need stability. The children, and they… The babe.'

'The child is four months old, is he not?'

She knew the ages of the children. And suddenly she understood. She had known his wife was dead, but not how. The Duke's wife had died giving birth. A realisation that made her own body tighten with remembered pain.

She had known his wife was dead but she had not paused to think of what that meant for him beyond the practicalities of the children.

She examined his face, looking for hallmarks of grief, but he was as unreadable to her in that regard as he had been when she was searching for the marks of a predator.

He was unreadable.

If he was remote and hard, then she could understand why. Loss she was familiar with. Perhaps not unto death, but it did not resonate in the soul differently. Not always.

She had lost her son.

She had given him away.

It had been a necessity.

And she did not often think of him.

But going into this household where there would be an infant, something she had not taken on as a governess yet, had put her mind in that place. It put her mind with that child. With the moment of his birth.

And his commentary on her accent had only exacerbated those thoughts.

'Yes,' he said.

He offered no further explanation.

'Your Grace,' she said. 'If I may, I am an accomplished student, and have proven to be an accomplished teacher when it comes to my charges. But I will also tell you, and you will have to forgive me if this is far too personal, that I have endeavoured to make a life for myself that is the essence of stability. Since we must speak of my past in Scotland, then let me assure you, I left because I was not afforded a life of stability there. I have sought to make one for myself. I would be happy to stay in one household for as long as I'm needed.'

'And you do not have designs on marriage?'

'No,' she said. 'I had the option to allow the Duke and his wife to sponsor me for a season. I declined.'

'Really? Very few women in your position would

have had that opportunity. Often, being a governess is a last resort.'

'It is not for me. I have chosen a life of education and occupation.'

'No yearning for a household or children of your own?' He did not ask it in a softer compassionate way, and it hit her as a knife's blade.

'None whatsoever. As I said, my life in Scotland was not one of stability. I have an overabundance of siblings. And falling somewhere in the middle, there was much care and keeping required of me.'

'Interesting that you would become a governess where you do care for children.'

'Under very different circumstances, Your Grace. But I imagine now this is much more information than you ever wanted to have about your governess. Just know that your priorities for your children are mine for my own life. I will endeavour to treat them as *your* own. Not my own. What you wish is what will be done.'

She never treated the children as her own. She did not open that section of her heart. She knew what it was to carry a child in her body. She had no desire to ever attach to her charges in such a way. And that was not what was required of her. It did not mean that she could not be kind, it didn't mean she did not care. But it was not the same as having a child of her own, and she was grateful for it.

For a governess had to leave her charges eventually. They grew up.

She would be with these children for much longer than she had been with the children of her previous household—should all things work out as she planned. She would care for them, but she would never love them. Not in that way.

It would be foolish, and it was certainly not something she could ever endure again.

She was being honest when she told him she had no desire for a husband or children.

She had no designs on men, not in that way. There was no mystery left to men, not for her.

She could not ever look forward to a wedding night the way a blushing bride might. In some ways, she counted herself lucky for that reason.

She was not a sad young woman forced into spinsterhood. She had chosen it. There was no great mystery to her when it came to men, and she was glad to have clear eyes.

She prized her freedom. Acknowledging that within the confines of society, as a woman, her freedom would always be limited.

She saw no merit in railing against this truth. Just as she saw no merit in bitterness. It wasn't that she didn't feel anger, she did, and she found it on occasion to be a powerful motivator. But bitterness…

Bitterness had turned her mother into a victim of

every circumstance. Bitterness had made her mother an ineffective champion for her daughter. For any of her children.

Bitterness saw you sitting down in the mud to die, to spite someone who never cared for you to begin with. And Mary refused to allow bitterness to dictate how far she could go in life. She had refused to sit in the mud. She had given up her child that he might have a better life, and if she did not go and pursue a better life for herself, then what was the purpose of the sacrifice?

She would have saved her child from the mud, only to consign herself to it, and she could not see the purpose in that.

And so while she might wander the earth with anger burning in her breast, she chose to make that into action.

Into change.

She did not rail against circumstances she could not alter. She moved in the world as it was, with clear-eyed pragmatism. One thing a life like hers did not afford was blind optimism or fate of any kind. She believed in what she could see. What she could touch. She did not secretly hope that humans might be better than their circumstances, better than the way the world had shaped them to be. Just as now she knew that the Duke was not acting with any sort of compassion. He was acting out of interest for his own convenience, and she would appeal to that.

Why try to appeal to his heart? She had yet to see evidence that men acted with their hearts. Yes, Lachlan, the leader of her clan, had acted with compassion. He was a good leader, and he used his position in the clan as that of a father. What he had done was what she had imagined a true father might have done for his daughter. Her own would have killed her.

But Lachlan Bain, leader of Clan McKenzie, was different. Still, she did not believe his actions came from his heart as much as it was inspired by his wife.

The sponsorship offer she had received from the Duke of Kendal had likewise been based on something other than emotion. It was a matter of honour for him, based on his connection to Penny, she was led to believe.

However they had behaved, the world was not run by the hearts of men, but rather the greed of them. And the desire for their own comfort, power and convenience. And this was the perspective by which she moved within the world.

'You will start immediately. But do not expect that you will be here long-term. It is likely the children will have run you out by day's end.'

His expression was cool, entirely neutral on his disturbingly pleasing face. His hair was dark, his eyes a shocking blue. His jaw was square, his chin strong.

His bearing of power, the mantle of strength that seemed to rest upon his broad shoulders, extended beyond the physical perfection, and yet the physical perfection of the man could not be ignored.

She could only be grateful that she would not see him. Not often. Eventually, most of her communication would be between herself and the housekeeper, she had no doubt.

A man of his status would hardly be interested in his children. As long as there was no issue, she imagined they would communicate largely through written report. And whatever he said, she did not foresee there being an issue.

He spoke of his children as if they might be feral beasts. But he had no idea. Her siblings had been quite literally feral. There had been no adult supervising their actions. They had been responsible for dressing themselves, feeding themselves. And often there had not been food. They had foraged for it. Begged for it.

Before Lachlan had returned to Clan McKenzie, life had been very dark. Circumstances in the Highlands were difficult. Poverty was more common than not.

And that was something she knew the Duke of Westmere would never understand. It did not matter how difficult his children were. It did not matter that she was in a working position, which would be perceived as being low by many. In her work she could be comfortable. In her work she always had food. She always had clothing. She was part of the household, she was protected.

She had set out to build a life that would insulate her in ways her upbringing never had. Never could.

Children, no matter how difficult or wild due to the loss of their mother, would never be a deterrent. Not when she knew what was actually waiting out in the rest of the world for young women.

Miss Mary Smith was a pragmatist, because Mary McLaren had been a victim.

She would never be that girl again. Not ever.

'Then let us go to the nursery.'

Chapter Two

West could not say why he was taking the trouble to show the new governess to the nursery himself. He could have transferred the task to Mrs Brown, and he should have.

The governess was far too pretty for his liking.

What should disturb him most was her lies. The Scottish accent beneath her English vowels. The deliberate attempt to obscure her origins.

But that was not what filled him with disquiet.

She wore a gown that was not quite the fashion, the waistline a bit too high. She had a fichu in place to cover the swell of her bosom, and yet somehow it had only served to highlight the lushness of her body.

She was pale, with striking red hair. The sort of beauty that would stop a man on the street.

She had not been speaking with vanity when she had claimed she could make more money as a mistress than a governess.

She had spoken only the truth.

He had reacted to that truth, to the image it painted. Physically. And he did not take any joy in that.

But she was such a strange, plainspoken woman.

He could hear the hint of a brogue beneath her words, though it was very carefully concealed.

It didn't surprise him that most people that she spoke to did not hear it. Most people believed what was being presented to them. He did not. He never had.

He was a man who looked beneath the surface.

A man with his power and his tastes, in life and in the bedroom, had to be discerning.

As if there was any point or benefit thinking about the bedroom now.

He had not been with a woman in some time.

And he certainly should not be thinking of such things around his newest employee.

He was a man of propriety and practicality.

He had very clear lines drawn in his life.

He kept appropriate distance between himself and his staff. He knew many men who saw their own household as their personal hunting grounds.

It was, to his mind, deeply distasteful. And he was never distasteful.

West was appropriate in all things.

And in all ways.

For all the good it had done these last months. His children were coming undone, and the babe...

He could not bring himself to touch the infant.

The child who did not have a name.

He was not christened…

It was true he was failing in this regard, and yet…

The child was responsible for the death of Jane. It was that simple.

And you don't think that you bear any responsibility for it…?

He gritted his teeth.

'We shall make our way upstairs. Elizabeth and Michael are under the care of the housekeeper at the moment. Mrs Brown will be able to give you all of the information that you may need regarding their routines, their likes and dislikes.'

'Do you not know these things?'

He did. He looked at her. 'Of course not.'

He said it to wrangle her, and he did not know why he wished to do so. Perhaps because she had surprised him. And he did not like being surprised.

'Yes. Of course.'

'How was the household run that you were employed at previously?'

'I never spoke to the Earl.'

'And yet you expect that I should be more deeply involved?'

The implication, of course, being that he was infinitely more important than an earl.

'The Earl had a wife.'

'As did I until four months ago.'

The change was jarring.

The children…

Everything with Jane had been difficult in the end anyway, and the children had been coming apart like stuffed toys with loose threads even before her death. Because they had known. Of course they had. The way things were changing. Shifting. How indeterminable things had come between their parents.

He did his best as a father.

He tried to give them guidance without ever causing harm. His own father had been a tyrant whose every mood had overflowed and flooded everything around him. West believed in boundaries. Gulfs. Trenches that kept all of his inclinations flowing in their appropriate streams.

He loved his children. It was the reason he observed formality with them. Guidance without corporal punishment. Respect without intimidation. Love, he imagined, in the same way God loved His children.

Distant.

He kept his visits confined to mornings and evenings, and always within a set timeframe.

But this was testing him. Beyond anything he had ever endured before. It was harder and harder to maintain those visits, and at the same time harder to maintain his distance as their behaviour shifted to intolerable.

The home was palatial, most of it finely upheld details from the early sixteen-hundreds, when his family had first constructed the estate. This portion of the house, which contained the children, and had also been where Jane's suite of rooms was housed, had been updated. He did not like it. But it had been his late wife's wishes to have some of her tastes considered in the decorating of the house.

Anger burned in his stomach.

Rage.

It would be time to go out and ride his horse in the countryside. Perhaps do a bit of target practice. Archery or guns, he was not particular. It may even be time to go into London and take his place in the ring at the boxing club he enjoyed.

The thought pushed against the back of his mind.

There were other pleasures he might make use of in London.

Things he had gone without for some time, and which may be a necessary release.

No.

He was not considering that, and most especially not while standing next to Miss Smith.

She was silent, for her part, as they moved down the endless marble corridor. He had not been in many of these rooms in years. When he came to visit the children, he went straight to the nursery. Never to their bedrooms.

And never to any of the other rooms here.

Jane could have been hiding any number of lovers in these rooms, how would he have ever known?

He gritted his teeth.

It was, he thought, a strange thing, that a man in his position should have dominion over so much. Should be in charge of a massive estate, the safety and wellness of everyone who resided under his care, a seat in Parliament, and yet could be entirely ignorant of what was occurring in his own home. In fact, it almost necessitated he be ignorant of what was going on in his home.

He had accepted that fact. For all of these years. Because he believed in keeping things contained.

A fire, after all, was only dangerous when it left the confines of the fireplace. His father had been a wildfire.

Burning everything he touched.

Destroying it all.

He had vowed his own passions would never burn the innocent.

'This is where the children spend most of their time?'

Miss Smith spoke for the first time since leaving his study. 'Yes,' he said. 'The nursery contains the toys, and classroom. Their bedrooms are in the adjacent rooms. I like for them to go outside, at least once every day. It is preferable that they take lunch outdoors, weather permitting. Even if the weather is unpleasant, I feel that they should dress for it and go outside. It does no good to become soft, even if money and title would permit.'

He believed in trying to make a hardy constitution for his children.

If Miss Smith had an issue with this edict, she said nothing. Which likely meant she didn't, as she had certainly not been hesitant to speak out when they had been in his study.

In normal circumstances he would've dismissed her. But these were not normal circumstances. He was desperate for a governess, and she was benefiting from his desperation. He did not like to admit weakness or vulnerability of any kind, but Mrs Brown was refusing to watch the children, as they more often than not resembled demons these days.

As if on cue, a large thump came from the room at the end of the hall.

'And what was that?'

He stopped and turned to her. And he felt his lips move. Felt his mouth curve up into a smile, even though he did not feel any mirth inside of his chest. 'The children.'

Then he strode forward, gripped the golden handles on the doors and opened them wide. Inside was a melee. Mrs Brown was standing in the corner observing the chaos as if it was a personal affront, not just to her but to all of society.

Elizabeth was standing next to a very lovely miniature version of the dining table that they had downstairs, which had been overturned onto its side.

A chair, robin's egg blue, with gold details, behind her was turned over onto its back.

Michael was next to…

Well, the remnants of a stuffed bear. Ironic, considering that he had only just thought of the children as fraying toys.

Michael was howling.

There was always something inside of his chest that rattled when his son did that. Or his daughter.

He had never made a noise above a whisper when his father was present. He had not wanted to do anything to attract his wrath.

He wanted to stop them when they did things like this, and he wanted to protect them. It was the strangest sensation, fighting inside of him like two dogs fighting over a piece of meat.

Anger and fear. Two sides of a very similar coin.

'You will be silent,' he said.

The children obeyed him, immediately. They looked up at him, and he could not discern the expression on their faces.

Were they afraid of him? He had never put his hands

on them, not once. But he did know that his expression could be formidable. His entire countenance, in fact.

He had been told so. Frequently.

Jane had been soft with them. And he had appreciated that. For all that they might have had their conflicts, their quarrels, Jane had been a wonderful mother. Loving. She had no problems demonstrating affection, physically and emotionally. He had considered her, in that way, a helpmeet. She had possessed something that he did not, and it was greatly appreciated.

And gravely, greatly missed.

'This is Miss Smith,' he said. 'She is to be your new governess.'

He could've sworn that when his daughter smiled her teeth looked sharp. 'I will tolerate no disrespect of Miss Smith,' he said.

Her smile fell just slightly. Good. He did not need her concocting new ways to scare off a governess. There had been spiders in tea, there had been mice put into slippers. Shoe polish in cosmetics, and on it went.

He might have been proud of the innovation of it if it was not so wholly and catastrophically inappropriate.

Your father kept you in line. Perhaps what you remember as a house of horrors was what was necessary in order to keep the devil child in line.

He dismissed that thought.

He would not beat his children. He would not leave

them outside all night to contend with the elements. A picnic in the afternoon in a drizzle was one thing.

His children would never fear for their lives.

And if they harassed a few more governesses because he refused to rule them with an iron fist, then so be it.

'Hello,' she said, her voice mild and pleasant. He didn't mind the hint of Scotland, he decided then.

It was different.

Her voice rolled over certain words pleasantly. Melodically. The brogue itself was gone, but there was a rhythm that was very different from a typical English accent.

The children ignored her.

'Elizabeth,' he snapped. 'Michael. Greet Miss Smith as she has greeted you.'

'Hello,' both children muttered.

'It is very nice to meet you,' she said. 'How old are you, Elizabeth?'

'I'm eleven,' she said.

Far too old to be throwing tantrums and overturning tables, but he did not say that.

'And you, Michael?'

'I'm eight,' he said stoutly.

He noticed a subtle shift in Miss Smith's facial expression. 'That's very nice,' she said. 'Very good ages.'

'They are not,' said Elizabeth. 'It's a horrible age.'

Miss Smith seemed to think about this for a moment. 'All right. If you insist.'

Elizabeth clearly didn't know what to do with that. She blinked, and frowned, but had no rejoinder.

'And the babe?'

'He's sleeping,' Elizabeth said.

'I'm sorry,' she said. 'I don't know what his name is. I seem to have forgotten.'

'He doesn't have one,' said Michael, not looking up.

'Oh,' said Miss Smith. 'I…' She looked up at him. Asking a question with her eyes.

'He doesn't have a name,' said Elizabeth. 'Because he killed our mother.'

This, he decided, would be the thing that drove her out of the room if she was easily frightened. Because these were the sorts of things his children said. Sometimes after turning over tables and tearing apart toys. This time it seemed they had done it as a prelude to chaos.

These were the sorts of things *he* felt. And fought. And if he were eight and eleven he might very well have turned over some tables himself.

'What do you call him, then?' she asked, her voice even.

'I don't speak about him,' said Elizabeth deliberately.

'And you, Michael? Do you speak about him?'

He shook his head. Then bent down and grabbed

the dismembered animal and began to pick stuffing out of one of the exposed holes. 'No.'

'I have work to do,' West said. 'I trust that I can leave you to sort out the rest of their day.'

Miss Smith was suddenly brisk, and all business. 'Yes. Of course. Everything is in hand.'

She was not bright, or overly cheerful, which was good; their last governess had been far too bright, a couple of years younger than Miss Smith seemed to be, and exceedingly irritating.

There was a no-nonsense aspect to her tone, and he found that he appreciated that. Along with her lack of reaction to this entire situation.

It remained to be seen if she would last even through the day.

If she did not leave of her own accord, then this evening when he called her to account in his study would be when his decision was made.

He had not had a room readied for her, and it had not been by accident.

He did nothing by accident.

She had been neutral upon meeting the children, her lovely face schooled into a blank slate.

He had a feeling her lack of response was practised. She had been free with her speech in his study. But he refused to accept criticism from a country spinster who had no idea what sorts of responsibilities were required of a man in his position. Who had no idea of the intricacies one navigated in a marriage and, most of all, when it came to children. It was not for her to comment. She would be useful for as long as she was useful, and when she was no longer useful she would be gone.

No matter how pretty or compelling she might be.

The problem, as far as West could see, with compelling things was that they often had nothing to do with duty. And there was no place to put that fascination.

If he had no place for something, it simply didn't belong. And he did not hesitate to excise it from his life.

Chapter Three

Michael looked up at Mary with angry blue eyes, from where he sat at the table with a pen clutched tightly in his fist.

She had known the moment she had walked into the nursery that she was doing battle with worthy opponents. But she was a no-nonsense governess, and in the end the children came to love her for it. Violet and Charlotte, her previous two charges, had been flighty girls who had not seen the merit in doing school work when they were only going to be married one day. But she had managed to get them to take their facts and figures seriously.

She could wrangle difficult children.

When she had sent Violet and Charlotte away from the classroom and into the ballroom, they had been flawlessly accomplished in manner, and in their minds. She would do the same with Elizabeth and Michael.

She understood that they were going through a difficult time, and what they needed was structure. Security. They had been through four governesses in the months since they had lost their mother. And even if they might have been part of pushing those women away, it was also keeping them in a state of instability, whether they understood it or not. She did.

Mary was an immovable object.

She thought of the Duke's blue eyes. The stubborn set of his jaw.

If she was an immovable object, the man was a mountain.

He might be formidable, but she herself had been accused of that a time or two. And she would win this. In the end, she would win. She would prove to the Duke that her past was not a barrier to her being an accomplished employee. Better, she would prove to him that her past was irrelevant, and that the real reason she chose not to share it was that it simply didn't matter.

Who she had been, that had nothing to do with who she was now.

It was nothing.

She rolled her sleeves up, grateful that the children were to be her only focus. If for some reason the wet nurse was unavailable she might have to step in, but Mrs Brown had presented that as a very unlikely possibility.

She did wonder why the Duke had not spoken of the babe.

Perhaps because it was not to do with her. But the children in this room were, and they required her focus.

'Is something amiss, Michael?'

'This is far too much schoolwork,' he said. 'The previous governess did not force us to do science. We only had to do the three Rs!'

'What a shame. It seems that the previous governess wasted much of your potential. But I will not. You can trust me to make sure that I'm giving you the very best.'

It was Elizabeth's turn to scowl. 'This doesn't matter to me!'

This was not the first time she'd had a female charge protest, and while she would ask her to explain herself, she already knew why. 'And why is that, Miss Elizabeth?'

'Because,' she said, 'I am a lady. And I will marry a gentleman.'

'I see. And you, Michael, you are the heir. Do you suppose that means you also don't need to learn?'

He sniffed. 'I'm not going to be a scientist. I'm going to be the Duke.'

'Yes,' she said. 'One day, you will be a duke.' Something he wouldn't become without the death of his father. She was certain he did not truly understand that now. 'But not today. And so, do you not think that perhaps in the time between this day and the day when you become the Duke, this day and the day when you become a man's husband, you may want to broaden the scope of your minds?'

'Why?' Elizabeth asked. It was not a genuine question, rather it was a mutinous one.

'Because life has a way of taking twists and turns we don't expect, and we never know what situations we may find ourselves in. When out in the natural world, a general knowledge of science is useful. When this estate is yours,' she said to Michael, 'will you not wish to know the names of the plants growing here? When you must balance the sheets, for the farmers, for those paying rent, for the rest of the household budget, will you not need to know your figures?'

'And me?' Elizabeth asked.

'What sort of man does your father intend to match you with? A *clever* man? A *kind* man? Or simply a titled man? As a woman, you are putting a great deal of confidence in a man you have never met before to ensure that your life runs as you would like it to. If you cannot carry knowledge for yourself, then you surrender all to this man whose name you do not even know.'

Elizabeth was eleven. She would be in the ballrooms hunting for a husband soon enough. She was a child now, yes, but a girl could not afford to ignore the realities. The practicalities.

Men controlled them. Everything they were allowed to have, and everything that they could achieve. They had to seize as much knowledge as possible for themselves. They had to understand that, with clear eyes.

They had to see it.

The world would say that Michael needed the education most, but she knew in her heart that it was Elizabeth who needed to be clever, who needed to understand the workings of things. If she married a man who was smart, who treated her well, then those things would be assets to her regardless.

But if she married an idiot, a man who mismanaged funds, a man who was cruel to her, then education, knowledge of the world, some understanding of the way that things worked outside of England, or simply an idea of how to manage money, to survive if she had to run, those things could save her life.

Perhaps Elizabeth, at eleven, could put her faith in a nameless, faceless suitor, but Mary would not do so on her behalf. It was the thing she valued most in her work. She ensured the girls in her care would be able to take care of themselves if need be.

That their minds were broad. That they knew more than simply the matters of hearth and home. Of manners and needlepoint. Pretty languages.

Elizabeth looked disquieted by what Mary had said. 'Husband is supposed to take care of you. Like Father...'

'Yes,' she said. 'If the world works in its ideal fashion, that would be so. But it is not always so. I do not say this to frighten you. You are very fortunate children. You were born with money. Your father is influential. What he says, what he thinks, it matters. And so what you say and think and want will also matter. But far better to understand the richness of this world that you occupy. Arithmetic, science, mathematics, art. Music. History, Geography and language, all of these things will give you that. And they will give you control. Power. That is what an education is. It is not simply hours spent in a schoolroom. It is options. Unfolding before you as far as you can see.'

She was not certain if her speech moved them, but they did sit down and begin to work with less complaint.

They did not go outside today—though she intended to make walks in the fresh air part of their routine once they had learned not to spend half the lesson time moaning at her.

They took supper, then the children were bathed, and were sent to bed.

And Mary was left on her own…and realised she had not been given a bedchamber.

She was standing in the centre of the long corridor, staring at the busts that lined the hall. In that moment, they felt as if they might be her only friends. She wondered if she would ever know the names of each of these figureheads. Did the Duke of Westmere in fact know who they all were? She imagined he did. And perhaps went and thanked each one of them every night for their place in his lineage.

He seemed the sort. To know everything. To feel a sense of gravity in all things.

Mrs Brown appeared at the end of the hall, her hands clasped tightly in front of her. The other woman was perfectly starched at all times, from her neatly pinned brown hair that was shot through with grey all the way down to her black skirts. She made Mary feel like her façade was poorly constructed indeed. 'Miss, the Duke respectfully requests that you join him in his study.'

Perhaps she was to be dismissed after all.

Perhaps all he'd needed was for her to stay the day.

She felt a rush of emotion that made her head swim and made her knees feel weak.

She knew two things in that moment.

She wanted to run from this place as fast as her legs could carry her.

And she would be devastated to never see the children again.

To never see the Duke of Westmere again.

Today, the children and her past had occupied her thoughts, but the moment she thought of the Duke it was like everything fell away but the vision of his stern blue gaze.

She should *want* to run from all of it.

That was wise.

But the feeling of sadness at the thought of leaving

was a strange sort of foolishness she could scarcely comprehend.

'Yes, ma'am,' she said, her heart thundering ever so slightly as she made her way down the stairs towards the location of the Duke's study.

She had assumed he would want a written account of the day, but it had not occurred to her that he would demand to see her again.

It made her stomach feel like a bellows with all the air pushed out.

So she focused on her surroundings. Her footsteps on the hard marble floor.

The wallpaper in this part of the house was garish. Bright green with creeping vines on it. It was such a bright green it was nearly cheerful.

It mocked her.

There was nothing cheerful in her heart, not now.

There was only dread, turmoil and the vision of the Duke's uncompromising face.

Her focus was so narrow now. Not on the past, not on the children. But on the man himself.

She had worked for two other families that were part of the aristocracy. And though they were not dukes, they had been important men. With wives who were well-positioned in society.

Perhaps it was the pall of grief cast over this house.

The Duke had just lost his wife. The children had just lost their mother.

It was a terrible thing.

And she should not judge them so.

She made her way to the door of his study and opened it slowly, stepping inside. He was sitting at his desk, just as he had been this morning, a quill in his hand and his eyes downcast on a paper before him. When he looked at her, the only thing that shifted was those eyes. Blue and piercing.

'Miss Smith.' There was something about his voice. She did not simply hear him speak her name, she felt it.

'Your Grace.'

'I wish to hear an account of the day. Which lessons did the children complete? And how do you find their proficiency?'

'Is that all you wish to know?'

'There is nothing else that matters.'

'They did French, mathematics and Latin. Elizabeth worked a bit on needlepoint. Tomorrow I should like to take them outside to get some fresh air. I should like to have them do some exercises.'

'Do whatever you see fit.'

'I shall want to have a rope ladder erected in the back garden.'

'Pardon me?'

'For exercise. It is good for strength, balance and the lungs.'

He lifted a brow. 'Do you...climb rope ladders?'

'I certainly do not ask the children to engage in activities I find impossible to complete.'

'Fair of you.'

'I strive for fairness at all times, Your Grace.'

His eyes went sharp. They might as well have been daggers. 'Even when lying to gain an employment position?'

She straightened. 'I did not lie to gain the position. I presented only the information that matters to the position.'

'Scotland does not matter?'

'Not to me.'

'And yet it must, or why keep it a secret?'

She sniffed. 'I told you, an accent would be a barrier to my finding work, unless that accent was French. I acclimatised to my surroundings, and is that not what we all do?'

'No. I was born to this.'

'You were not born standing upright and wearing a black suit. Your Grace.'

The corner of his mouth curved upward, and she had the terrible sense that he felt he'd won some sort of victory.

She imagined herself standing in very soft mud. Imagined her heels digging in completely.

'All of us play a role,' she said. 'I play the role which most benefits myself and my charges.'

He thumbed through a stack of papers on his desk,

very deliberately putting his attention there, until his eyes went sharply to hers. 'I am Westmere. There is no becoming. No playing. I was born to it. For it. Everything I have, everything I have inherited, has bent itself around me.'

'And how nice for you,' she said. 'But the world has not been so accommodating to me. So I must bend. I have. I will continue to do so in order to keep this position, but I will not be made to feel ashamed of myself for doing what was necessary.'

She had stepped over the line again, she was certain.

'Are you always so forthright?'

'No,' she said.

She wasn't. There was something about him. Normally, she spoke to housekeepers, and perhaps the children's mother. But no one had ever demanded a full account of what the children had done in the day, least of all in such an emotionless manner.

'I do not require your shame,' he said. 'I simply wish to know the woman minding my children.'

'It might be beneficial for you to have some personal involvement with your children.'

Another icy glare, and this one she felt in the pit of her stomach.

'Do you mean to scold me for how I handle my own children?'

As far as she could see he did *not* handle the children.

'They are struggling. This has been a very tumultuous time…'

'Do you not think I am aware of that? Why do you think I've had four governesses leave in as many months? Because the children are angry. But I am angry as well. And there is not much that I can do. They can yell at their governess, and what am I to do? Rage at God?'

She felt some sort of secret satisfaction at this. At this unravelling of the contained man before her. Not a complete unravelling, but a loose thread had been revealed. It made her feel as if she had more power than she had a moment before, and yet she could hardly feel too triumphant having used his children and the death of his wife to get a response from him.

'I find sometimes it is necessary to do so,' she said. 'And that God has broad shoulders. He can certainly bear the burdens that we place upon him.'

'And now you speak to me of God?' The words were hard.

'You spoke to me of him first. I thought this was a conversation.'

He stared at her. And she knew that he found her utterly insolent.

She spoke to him as she had his children. She found it easier.

'I am terribly sorry, Your Grace. It is perhaps that I am near feral, not being English.'

'You are certainly not English.'

His face was a study in hard granite lines.

He was...

He was starkly beautiful. She would guess the man to be nearing forty. There was grey at his temples.

He was angry, and yet he kept that anger leashed. She could sense it, boiling beneath the surface of his skin, and yet he did not give it free rein. Nothing like her father, who had led with his fists, his brandy-induced rages a terror for his wife and children.

And then there was the man who had attacked her. Useless. Nothing. The sort of man who wanted nothing more than to prove his strength by breaking someone weaker than him.

Pity the man who did not understand what the strength of the heart looked like.

Perhaps pity was the wrong word. Because she did not pity him at all. She hoped his soul rotted in the depths of hell.

It was said that forgiveness set one free.

She did not believe in bitterness. She did not believe in forgiveness for the unrepentant either. The lake of fire would suffice.

And she wished him well in it. So that he could survive longer with the flames licking his skin.

'You will understand that the household has been in a period of mourning.'

'I do, Your Grace. And yet your children should be in a position of importance.'

'It is not a matter of importance. It is a matter of what can be endured. My wife is dead. As you can see, the children miss her. And I am not her. Nor will you be.'

'Did the children spend most of their day with a governess before?'

'Parts of the day. Jane, for her part… The Duchess, I mean. The Duchess. She spent a great deal of the day with them.'

She felt herself soften at the mention of the former Duchess's Christian name. Had the woman lived, he would not have referred to her so, not in conversation with Mary.

Had the woman lived, she would not be here talking to him.

'She sounds like a lovely woman.'

'She was. Nurturing and lovely and a brilliant mother.'

Her heart squeezed tight. He had loved her. Greatly.

She could only imagine what it must be like to be loved by such a man. To be loved by anyone.

She had been given great care. By Penny and Lachlan. By the Duke of Kendal, distant though it was.

But she had never been loved. And she was well aware of that.

This man, this hard man, had, with all of his considerable strengths, loved this woman, and it had sent him into a terrible grief that made it impossible for him to even name his own child. It was unfathomable.

It was beautiful and terrible all at once.

But it was the envy that nearly swallowed her whole that shocked her.

What would it be like to have male strength used to protect her in such a way?

She had been avenged. That was the truth.

But Lachlan had avenged her as much out of rage for what had happened to her as out of the need to protect the clan. The need to show himself their leader.

He had made sure that it was known to all that rape was not tolerated in Clan McKenzie, and that the penalty would be death. Outright.

A crime that was overlooked in many places in the world, and certainly in many parts of the Highlands, would be dealt with swiftly and brutally in Clan McKenzie.

It had been for her. But it had very much been for the order of the clan.

Very much.

She was not angry about that.

It was only that she had to wonder…

As she thought about it, memories of being held down assaulted her. Memories of struggling against a man's strength.

Men had strength, all of them. What would it be like to be held in security? In care?

To have that strength used differently.

She realised she was staring at him, and that her breath had gone shallow.

His hands were large, still gripping that quill, and she had difficulty looking away from him.

'I am sorry,' she said. 'It is a terrible loss.'

'Yes, it was.'

'Tomorrow, shall I report back to the same place?'

'Yes.'

'Your Grace...' She took a breath. 'I have not been given a room.'

His brow lifted. 'I had not decided if you would stay.'

'And now?'

He appraised her, swift and stark. In a way that made her feel peeled of all her layers. It was no different than the way he had appraised her earlier in the day, but perhaps because of how long the day had been and how deeply it had tried her emotions, she found she had no defence against it.

He stood up from behind the desk, and she fought the urge to shrink away.

He was not the sort of man she had the need to be afraid of, but there was something imposing about his presence all the same. It was... A shock to her senses. Because it was entirely foreign to her. The way that he made her feel. There were men who made her feel hunted. Men who made her feel ready to scratch and claw and bite.

She kept a knife in her corset. And there were men who made her feel as if she might need to retrieve it.

He was not one of those men.

There were men who put her at ease. Men who did not set off alarm bells in her soul.

They were strong, yes, and large, but they were not the sort of man who had any use for testing that strength against others. This was something else altogether. His presence seemed to fill every corner of the room.

His presence seemed to reach inside of her and lift her lungs, her heart, her stomach, straighten up her posture. It seemed to fill her. Consume her.

She could not look away from his face. The masculine lines there, deep grooves between his eyebrows, bracketing his mouth.

And then there was his physique. His shoulders were broad. He was impossibly tall, making her feel small.

He made her heart beat faster.

And not from fear.

God in heaven, how she wished it were fear.

He was, she had the feeling, the strongest and most physically fit man in most rooms. And perhaps that was why he seemed so uninterested in testing that strength. He had no need.

He rounded the desk and came to stand in front of her. And for some reason the intensity of his gaze made her want to lower her eyes.

She found her gaze fluttering down to the floor.

'I shall have Mrs Brown accompany you.'

She looked up from beneath her lashes. 'That won't be necessary. If you can simply give me directions.'

'You will not be able to find it. This place is labyrinthine.'

She was suddenly deeply aware that they were alone. And yet she had the sense that he would only ever protect those in his care. She did not know why she had that sense. He had not been kind to her, not especially, nor was he warm to his own children.

There was, quite honestly, no reason to assume such a thing about him. And yet she did.

When her gaze met his, there was something hot, banked fire in the blue, and it made her throat go dry.

'You did well today.'

There was something about the assurance that felt as if each word had released something within her. A contentment rolled through her body, relaxing everything that had lifted a moment before.

'I am fair,' he said. 'And I give praise when it is due. If you do well, I will not withhold approval.'

She searched for a tart reply and could not find one.

It felt as if she had lost. And still, the only words she could find were, 'Thank you, Your Grace.'

'Tomorrow. I will see you in this very spot.'

'Yes, Your Grace.'

Chapter Four

The sharp knock on his study door was a full two minutes earlier than expected. He had a feeling she was early on purpose.

He had thought about her today, while he had seen his correspondence, fielding requests from his wife's cousin to come for dinner.

He had no good reason to refuse, and so had dashed off a response, and was certain that he could expect them at the end of the week.

But she had stuck in his mind.

The way that she had responded to him last night when he got too close to what she didn't wish to speak of. She was guarded, and he wanted to get beneath that defence.

She worked for him, and he needed to know the manner of woman caring for his children.

It was not because one look from her green eyes was like the point of a blade digging beneath his skin.

It was not because the vision of her face had been with him over the course of the day.

'Come in.'

The door opened, and when she walked in it was as if the study became more vibrant. Her red hair was pinned back ruthlessly, and she was wearing a green dress which was yet again just a bit outside of fashion. He wondered if she had bought new clothing when she had first joined the Earl's family and had not made any replacements since. He knew enough about women's fashion. His wife had been perfectly dressed at all times. The height of fashion. Her dark hair always arranged perfectly and wearing only colours that set off her particular brand of beauty.

Jane had caught his attention from the very first moment he'd seen her. If only that had been enough.

'You're still here,' he said.

'Where else would I be?'

'My children have driven out every other governess they've had since the death of their mother. I have no reason to believe that you will be any different.'

Her green eyes became hard like emeralds. Glittering and profoundly beautiful. 'I am different.'

'What do you have to report for the day?'

She looked to the side, and then walked towards one of his bookshelves. Her movements were slow and deliberate. The set of her shoulders was proud, like a soldier. The issue with the way she wore her gowns was it made it very difficult to get an idea of the shape of her body. Her breasts were generous, he could see that much, but the full skirts flowed too easily over the rest of her curves. The garment she wore beneath the gown concealed her skin where he might enjoy the sight of her lush bosom.

She was his employee, and he should not have these thoughts.

He never had before. He was not simply controlled in action, but in everything else. He did not even struggle with temptation, so ruthlessly had he divided his life into segments.

So deeply did he know the rules.

She was smooth, and utterly contained today, and he resented that. More than he could say.

It made him want to push.

Yesterday, he had succeeded in angering her, and when he had, some of that composure had fractured.

She talked back to him. No one did that. Not a single person who worked for him, no one in society, not even Jane.

It was novel. And at the moment felt somewhat essential.

'Michael had a very difficult day today,' she said finally.

'In what sense?'

His son had always been a spirited boy, but something had changed when his mother had died. It was no longer running through the halls or attempting to slide down banisters. It was anger, the energy expressing itself in outbursts.

'He had a fit of rage that lasted quite some time. We will need to replace some furniture in the nursery.'

Her expression remained placid. If she was angry, frightened or upset by what had happened, it did not show on her face.

'And you are still here,' he said.

'The anger of a child deep in the throes of mourning does not upset me. What upsets me is not knowing how to help. Do you know...'

'I do not know.' Whatever she was going to ask, he had no answer. For how could he? How could he know what to do with a little boy? He had his own complicated, painful emotion surrounding the loss of Jane, what was he supposed to do with the child?

'You are his father.'

'Yes. I am. But that has little to do with knowing what to do with the child who has suffered a loss. You are his governess, that is your business.'

'You are his father. You should know him.'

'I do not know this version of that child. I do not know this version of my life.'

He had meant to push at her, and instead, she had flicked that emerald knife blade right beneath the skin. Instead, she had upended him.

And she would pay for that.

'I think they might need to speak of their mother. I need some tokens, something, to introduce the conversation, but I did not know the woman, and I am not certain how I would speak to that. Perhaps it needs to come from you.'

'Do not seek to tell me how to be a father to my children. I am constant. And I have not changed. Do you not think that perhaps that is what they need the most?'

'I think perhaps they may need love the most. You said yourself, your wife was warm, she spent time with them. Perhaps what they miss is—'

'It is a woman's touch that they miss.'

'You speak with such authority, but you don't see what happens in the nursery. I do.'

'You've been here for two days. Do not speak to me as if you have a deeper knowledge of this than you do.'

'Am I now too competent at my job?'

'Did I say that?'

'You say that I cannot know these things after two days, but you insist on vetting me. You say that you are only concerned with having the best person for your children, and yet you doubt me when I display confidence.'

'I have done no such thing.'

'You have. Tell me, is it all of your employees, or only the women that must prove themselves to you beyond doing the work that they have been assigned?

You have asked for an account of my day, and you have asked for my opinions, and now you reject them.'

There it was. The spark. Her anger. It fuelled something in him. Ignited something in his gut. It made him feel like he was winning.

He stood up and rounded the desk. 'I fail to see how asking for an account of your day is an agreement that I will take everything you say as Scripture. I do not recall ever promising that it would be so.'

'I am only asking that you listen to me.'

'Is that what you are asking? Or are you asking that I take your every word without question, and then accuse me of discounting you because you are a woman, when I would never consider hiring anyone but a woman for this position. You are out of line, Miss Smith.'

'I am speaking a truth you do not wish to hear, Your Grace.'

He could dismiss her. He should dismiss her. No one should speak to him this way. No one had ever dared.

But dammit, it fired his blood, and it made him feel something other than the relentless, endless grey that had taken over his life.

She excited him. And that was better than anything else she might make him feel.

He wished to push her. Harder. He wished to get beneath her skin, to make her walls crumble.

He wanted to know her. She was a mysterious smooth box and he could not find his way in.

And it was better than the mystery of his children. The mystery of what he was to do with the life that he was left with.

'Your truth, perhaps. But at Attingham, the only truth that matters is mine. And I disagree. I think the children need you. Provided, of course, you are able to give them what they require. And if not, leave my study now, leave the estate now. Pack all of your things and do not stay another night.'

That incensed her. Regardless of how still she held herself, her anger was clear.

'I can care for your children. I told you, I am not bothered by Michael's moods, what I am bothered by is that there are no tools to help him. And certainly none coming from you.'

'Do you see this?' he asked, gesturing to his desk, to the papers there. 'I am responsible for the lives of many. I must manage the estate, and all those who depend on it, and that is when I am not in my seat at the House of Lords for matters of Parliament. I have many responsibilities, and you have one. It is to care for my children. Can I trust you to do that?'

'I am doing it.'

'Good. Then we will keep this to the confines of our meetings. You will do as you are instructed to do, and you will not return to this study with a list of tasks for me to perform. I set the standard. I set the boundaries. I set the rules. Are we clear, Miss Smith?'

She looked down for a moment, the lovely sweep of her lashes fanning over her cheekbones tightening his gut. And then when she looked back up at him, with that emerald brilliance, he felt the impact of it echo in his cock.

It was a base and undeniable reaction. He could excise his thoughts about her beauty as the vague observations of a man who was fond of beautiful women.

He could not excuse the abject lust that fired in his veins in that moment. Could not dismiss it as an aberration or the consequence of some time of celibacy.

It was specific. And it was about her.

The way she held her posture, the way she looked down, while he could still feel a fight brewing beneath her skin like a storm.

'Yes, Your Grace.' And then she looked up, her eyes meeting his at just the right moment.

It was like fire.

It was not supplication. Not truly. And there was something about that which felt like a challenge.

To make her say *yes* and mean it. To make her say *Your Grace* without the poison lacing each syllable.

To say it as a prayer.

He took a step back, rejecting those thoughts wholly. They did not fit within the confines he had created for his life. She did not fit in *his* rules, and yet he needed her here.

You want her here. Because she distracts you. She excites you.

He ignored that. He did not have to answer to anyone, least of all the interrogation of his own mind.

He was a duke, after all, and what good was it if he had to be subject to the whims of others, or answerable to anything.

He had a moral code, and he would follow it. He knew it so well now that he did not have to question his every action. And that was the point of it.

'You are dismissed, Miss Smith.'

'I bid you good evening, Your Grace.'

Chapter Five

Her heart was thundering hard when she left the study. She did not know what passed between them when they spoke, but it felt like something more than the words that they spoke, and she could not understand why.

Could not understand what. And yet it made her skin feel flushed, and her heart thunder.

It made her want to fight him. And she was aware that she crossed lines whenever she spoke to him, and yet she could not find a way to…

She could not find her shield. The icy governess was a worthy façade to hide behind, and yet with him it became something else. She had tried, just yesterday, to think of him as one of her charges, but it was not so simple. He was not a child.

He was a man.

And he was a man quite unlike any other she had dealt with. So she could not fall back on her designated ways of handling him.

It was distressing. Appalling.

She went up the stairs, her heart thundering heavily, and then she heard it. The sound of the infant crying.

She stopped.

It had been said to her that if the child needed care, it may occasionally fall to her.

She stood there. Her heart had already been beating far too fast, and now it was beginning to make her feel dizzy. Ill.

The babe...

She could not hold the bairn.

She had never held a bairn.

Never.

The wet nurse would come. She would.

And then she saw the woman racing down the hall, and did wonder why she had not been in residence with the child, but it was not her place to ask.

'Sorry, miss,' she said. 'I'll see to him.'

'Thank you,' she said, feeling frozen and stiff.

The woman disappeared into the nursery, and on numb feet Mary continued down the hall.

She walked into the chamber, undoubtedly the most beautiful room that had ever been hers. The bed was large, with silk brocade curtains around the outside. She liked them. They made her feel secure.

Slowly, she undressed, and as she did she thought of...

His blue eyes.

For some reason, she thought of them now. It made her skin feel hot, prickly.

She squeezed her eyes shut fiercely, stopped the movements of her hands, because her own hands made her think of his.

She had been afraid of men before. In the years since she had left Scotland. But she had never been afraid of herself. Of her own thoughts. But it was as if he had taken residence in her mind, it was as if he had done something to her, and she did not know how to get dominion of her own thoughts on her own body back.

Breathing hard, she stripped down the rest of the way and put on her nightdress, and then she got into bed, the curtains closed firmly around her. Enclosed in the dark box, one that should make her feel secure. But he was still there.

I am Westmere.

His voice echoed in her head and through her body, deep and affecting. It was the truth. He was in every brick, every stone statue, every dab of paint on canvas, he was in the air she breathed. He was all-consuming, all-encompassing in this home that might well have been his own personal kingdom.

She had not given him permission to inhabit her thoughts in this fashion. And she would not allow it to happen again.

Tomorrow, she would be nothing but impeccably

appropriate in her interaction with him. She would not allow him to get beneath her skin again. She refused. She took several deep breaths, and she bid herself to be calm. Tomorrow would be different. She would be different. She had reinvented herself once already, and she could change in whatever way she needed in order to survive this.

She needed thicker armour, that was all.

And she was more than up to the task of making it.

'Today,' she said, looking at her two angry charges, 'we will go for a walk.'

Elizabeth looked outside, her eyes going round. She had her father's eyes. If not precisely the colour, the uncompromising edge to them. 'It's raining.'

'So it is,' Mary said cheerfully. 'But this is England. And if we were to stay inside because of the rain, we might never go out.'

'I don't want to,' said Michael.

'But you need fresh air. We need to get some exercise. It is important. The building of a healthy constitution begins in childhood.'

She said this, confident that logic would prevail. It did not.

'I don't care,' said Elizabeth. 'I don't care what you think, and I don't care if I get exercise.'

'Then we should clean up the nursery,' she said.

The children looked at her as if she had grown another head. 'That is not our job,' said Michael.

'You seem appalled by the idea that you might have to clean something. Whose job is it?'

'Yours,' he said. 'Or one of the maids.'

'And why could you not clean the nursery?'

'It is a disaster,' said Michael, surveying the damage that he himself had done yesterday.

'And yet you find it acceptable that someone else should have to take responsibility for this. But it is a horrifying thought that you might. Come now, we will tidy the place, and we will do it together. If you will not take responsibility for the health of your bodies, you will take responsibility for your surroundings. You treated your things yesterday with an appalling lack of respect and care. Perhaps this will teach you...'

'No,' said Michael, sitting in the middle of the floor and gripping his toes, refusing to move. 'If my mother were here she would dismiss you.'

The truth of what he'd said settled around all of them. *If* his mother was here.

But she was not.

Mary was not unkind enough to say it. Michael was a child and he was lashing out. But she would speak truth to him, even if the edges of that truth were harsh.

'Perhaps,' she said softly. 'But *I* am here. And this is what I am asking you to do.'

Structure would help them. She was convinced of

that. In the end, stability, and her proving that she would not be held hostage to their moods, would make them feel safe. It would.

The Duke saw the rotation of governesses as a failure on their part, he saw it as misbehaviour from his children, but what he wasn't understanding was that it did not need to be punished, rather it needed to be proven ineffective. What the children needed was for the person caring for them to prove that they could not drive her away.

Their mother had gone away, and every person who had cared for them since had found their pain too much to bear. Their father did not come into the nursery, he had said that he spoke to them twice a day, and yet she had not seen him once.

Because of his own grief he avoided them, or maybe he always had, but the children had no one, and she would not be like that. She knew what it was to feel as if you could count on nothing. To wonder if those who were supposed to care for you would. She had also experienced the bitter truth of not receiving that care.

No, these children were not in danger of not having food. They were not in physical danger, but it did not mean they didn't feel imperilled in their hearts.

And it made her ache for them.

'We will begin to tidy now.'

'Not me,' said Elizabeth, sitting in a chair and crossing her arms.

'We will not be taking tea until this is finished. And I will not finish it on my own.'

'You can't do that,' Elizabeth protested.

'I am afraid that I can. Your father has put me in charge. Therefore, what I say and what I require of you is what is to be done.'

'But you can't! You can't! You can't!' Elizabeth stood, her cheeks fiery with rage. She stomped her foot with each statement, and the only thing Mary could think was that she hoped Elizabeth always retained that spirit. That none of the men in her life ever extinguished it. It would be a furious and wonderful thing for her to carry with her into her womanhood, though it would not make things easy for Mary now.

But she would always rather a woman had spirit. It would often be the only thing that might insulate her.

'I can, you will find. You do not command the servants. I do. And I will ensure that there is no tea until this is finished. I do not mind suffering alongside you, so if you think that you will break my will in that fashion, you are mistaken.'

Living with hunger was familiar for her. While she did not enjoy it, she knew how to be uncomfortable. She had spent the first thirteen years of her life in some sort of discomfort or another. Whether it be cold, damp, tired, hungry...

She never took surroundings like the kind she found at Attingham for granted.

It took an hour. An hour to get them moving. To get them to participate. But they did.

Tea was delayed by an hour, and she was desperately hungry by the time she sat down. They made it through the lessons, and even though they didn't make it outside that day she was proud of what had been accomplished.

She had stuck to what she said, she had not allowed them to take control of the situation, or to undo her. She had redoubled her efforts to find control last night, and it was worth it. Tonight, when she spoke to the Duke—and she had to ignore the swooping sensation in her stomach when she thought of him—she would be cool and collected, and entirely appropriate.

She ignored the way that her heart pounded as she made her way to his study. She knocked with confidence.

And when he bid her enter, she opened the door and went inside.

'Make your report,' he said, his tone brisk.

He was not looking at her. And that gave her a moment to examine him, his head bent over his papers. His shirtsleeves were rolled up, revealing forearms that spoke of physical labour. He was far more muscled than either of her previous employers, who had clearly enjoyed lives of leisure as granted them by their titles.

But not the Duke of Westmere.

Again, she thought the man was closer to mountain than human.

His hair was dark, left just long enough to curl in some places. Standing, you could not see that, but sitting like this with his focus on his papers, she could. There was grey at his temples, and some mixed throughout. It had an astonishing effect on his good looks, as did the lines on his face. They lent him an air of distinction and ruggedness. She could imagine that as a young man he had been stunning in his beauty, but thought that age had probably tempered that in the way of a well-aged wine.

She ought not to think about his features in such detail, but he commanded her focus. She was certain he was the sort of man who commanded the focus of all eyes in any room he was in.

She took a breath, remembering to focus on why she was here.

'It was a difficult day at the start of it, but I refused to be held hostage by them, and the end result was that they cleaned the nursery.'

He looked up, and she felt like he had struck her right through the heart with an arrow.

'My children are not household staff,' he said.

'No. But they are in desperate need of someone to show them that they need authority in their lives, and that authority will not bend, or abandon them.'

His face was like stone. 'My children do not need to be scrabbling around…'

'Your Grace,' she said, doing her best to keep her voice mild. She ran into trouble with him when she allowed him to get beneath her skin. 'They are fine. They completed their task. They had their tea. By the time supper came, they had forgotten entirely how furious they were with me. But I did not leave them, and that is the important part. Tomorrow, I imagine that when I suggest we go out for some exercise they will obey and easily. The consequence today was that they cleaned rather than doing so, as they refused me.'

'Their refusal of you is unacceptable.'

'Yes, I know. It stems, I feel, from the lack of stability in their life.'

'Is this another opportunity for you to lecture me?'

'I believe, Your Grace, that a lecture is only a lecture by the interpretation of the one who hears it. I do not seek to lecture you. Merely to explain my position. And as you have rejected my thoughts on what might help them feel that sense of stability, I must do the job myself.'

'That is what you were hired for.'

She looked past his head, at the shelves behind him, the dark wood absorbing all the light around them. The study was meticulously cleaned, but full, with centuries of history all right there. His family.

He was Attingham. He was Westmere.

He had told her this. She'd felt it last night. But now it pressed down upon her, made her feel small. Inconsequential. As if he had roots that went deep into the earth while she could fall at the slightest wind.

He was entrenched in his position. And she had fashioned hers from the air.

It was so very different.

And it was little wonder she did not know how to speak to him.

He was a man who had never had to concern himself with these things, because his wife had not only managed the governess, she'd managed the children. And now it was up to him. And yet none of his other responsibilities had abated. And she had to wonder just how much his own grief was closing him off as well. How much of this was the same as his son sitting in the middle of the floor and holding tightly to his feet, as if to try and contain every feeling inside of his body.

It gave her a measure of sympathy for him that she had not felt before.

He was a man surrounded by constancy. He must not know his life now. How had the world dared to go against him in this way? She wondered if it ever had previously.

She, in contrast, had never had stability of any kind. Whatever she had now, she'd created for herself, with this persona that she had made. She knew how to weather change. She knew that not all change was bad. And she knew that even when things were bad you could come out of it stronger.

He was a duke, yes, a man in charge of much, but she wondered if he knew these things.

For he was the estate, and the very history all around him and the busts that lined the halls were his kin. Unchanging. Set in stone.

'I think I might understand where we are conflicting with each other,' she said.

His eyes met hers. 'Do you?'

'Yes. Your Grace, your life has been a constant. I am now truly appreciating the depth of the history of your family. The traditions that are passed on, and how fixed it all must feel. When you were a child, did you have your mother?'

'Yes,' he said. 'Though I fail to see...'

'And so you never saw anyone navigate such a situation. You do not know what the loss of the mother, wife, looks like. I wonder if you even know what change looks like. I do. I have changed countries. And I understand what it means to start a life that feels entirely new. You are in need of a new perspective. Yes, before, you had to keep your focus solely on the estate. Because your children had a mother. And yes, before, your contribution was sufficient, but now I feel you must change your approach. Your life has changed, and therefore you must.'

And she could see then that she had miscalculated. She had thought to appeal to his heart, but what she saw burning in the depths of the blue in his eyes was frightening. Foreign and terrifying. And quite unlike anything she had ever experienced before. And it did something to her that was also outside of the realm of her knowledge. Her stomach tightened, and something low inside of her began to quiver.

She trembled.

But she was not cold.

He stood from his position behind the desk, as she had enticed him to do every night now. His presence filled the room, his great height nearly overwhelming.

He was physically imposing.

Terrifying and starkly beautiful all at once. And she was immobilised by it. By the perfection in the lines of his face, the grace with which he moved.

And the rage that radiated from him.

'I am the Duke of Westmere. What I am, what I am responsible for, does not shift with time. It is not built on sand. It is not something that will change with the wind. It is a rock. And though a piece has fallen away, I stand firm. You do not tell me what needs to be done in my own household. Have I not paid you sufficiently to manage these things for me? Do you not report to me that you have set my children to rights?'

'I got them to do what I needed them to today, but that does not mean...'

'Enough.'

He drew closer to her, so close that she could smell the scent of him. His skin, and something smoky. Tobacco, perhaps. He was clean, soap mingling with another scent, something masculine and raw.

The sort of thing that would normally have made her lash out. Or run.

And yet she did not run. She imagined herself standing in soft ground again, but this time it was not simply her heels that dug in. She felt as if her entire foot was weighted down there. Stuck to the spot. Grounded.

'Do you think you know better than I do?'

She could argue. It was what she had done yesterday, and it was what she had done the day before. And she nearly wondered if that was what he wanted. To spark her fury, because then it would give free rein to his.

He had not dismissed her over her impudence. And she had to wonder why.

It seemed to make him angry, and yet he seemed to almost want her to behave badly. So she decided to try something new. She would be the governess. She would be the employee that he needed her to be.

She did not respond. She kept her face placid. And he drew closer.

Her heart began to flutter like a trapped bird, and

yet more disturbing was the pulse that echoed between her thighs.

It confused her. And yet she could not let him see it.

That there was something about his strength she found compelling rather than terrifying. That even now, as he drew close to her, she did not feel threatened.

'Of course, Your Grace. I am sorry if I have stepped across the line. You have asked for an account of the day, and I seek to give it, along with what wisdom I feel I may offer based on what I've seen. But yours is the only real wisdom that must be taken into account.'

The banked flame behind his eyes did not abate. Rather it only seemed to glow with more intensity.

'You are my master,' she said.

She looked up then, their eyes colliding, and she could not account for what felt like a thunderclap between them.

Somehow, she had managed, with this game, to step into dangerous territory that she could not name or understand.

She liked it. That was the strangest thing. From the heat in his eyes to the satisfaction she felt naming him as her master by her own choice.

With those words she had given him power. Yes, society gave him power. His body granted him strength. She could do nothing about those things, could not fight them. But she could give him that.

Master.

And see what he did with it.

Test him.

Test herself.

She hadn't intended to. But now she'd done it.

He lifted his hand, and it hovered there between them. And she thought, wildly, that he meant to touch her.

But then he lowered it again and did not.

Her breath left her lungs in a gust, and she was sure that he would've seen that.

And now she felt afraid. Fighting with him did not scare her. But this... This draw she felt towards his authority, towards his strength, created a terror that rattled around inside of her, heedless and without authority. Save his.

She took a step back.

'When you call upon me tomorrow, I will make no more suggestions.'

'We will not meet tomorrow,' he said, turning away from her and going back to his desk.

'We...will not?'

She felt a rush of relief flood her. And sadness at the same time.

'My wife's cousin, the Earl of Blackwater, is paying a visit, along with his wife and some business associates. They are en route to Bath and decided it was time they paid personal respects. Upon the afternoon we will go out shooting, and then we will take dinner, after which I am certain conversation will run long.'

'Yes. Of course.' She did not know why she felt altered by this change. Why it felt like a loss. 'Then I will be sure to make a written account of the day and leave it on your desk.'

'A good plan.'

'Thank you, Your Grace.'

She nearly fled. She had no idea what was taking her over. She was a woman of unparalleled control. And men... Men did not...

She put her hand to her chest as she walked back to her room, pausing outside the nursery, her heart aching. Feeling bruised.

That was what happened when you let a man touch you. The babe.

The babe.

And for what? What?

It was all pain and fear and absolutely nothing to be offered to a woman. His wife had died. She had died having that babe.

Being in his bed had killed her.

And she knew that women did it every day. And did not die. Did not get with child. And now she knew how to prevent it, because she had made herself an expert on these things, in a desperate bid to understand.

But it did not...

The pull to him was unconscionable. Untenable.

She could not bear it. She could not allow that spark to turn into a flame.

She was twenty-two years old, and she had never looked at a man and found him beautiful.

She did not wish to do so now.

She went to her room and began to disrobe. Yes, he was beautiful.

This was what she needed to do. She needed to do with herself what she would do with one of the children experiencing a feeling they did not wish to have. You could not always deny things. Sometimes you had to take them out and examine them, turn them from a mystery into something less interesting.

As long as it was sitting there untried in the back of her mind she would see him and feel unsettled by these feelings.

He was a starkly beautiful man. There were few who would deny that to be true.

Her reaction to him was simply down to the fact that she was unfamiliar with thinking so.

But it was an everyday occurrence for a woman to look at a man and find him pleasing to her eyes. It did not mean she needed to draw closer to him. It did not mean he looked at her and thought she was beautiful.

It did not have to connect with activities in the bedroom. It did not.

She would never touch him. That she looked at him and saw beauty was simply down to the fact that he was beautiful. Like looking at a sunset. An ocean.

It was not special. And it did not have to mean more than that.

She would look at him from now on and think he was no more than a sunrise. A thing to be enjoyed, certainly, but nothing that you could possess, and nor should you want to.

There. She had accepted it. Admitted it. And put it in its place. And she would be free of all the unwanted feelings she could not begin to untangle.

Her thoughts about his strength. The way that he had looked at her when she had said he was her master.

These things would vanish. She was confident of that.

Chapter Six

It had been a long while since he had received visitors. He was not especially in the mood.

He had never been overly fond of his wife's cousin, but the Earl of Blackwater was family, and he did not feel it appropriate to deny him an audience.

He came with three men West had done business with before—Lord Pelham, who was tall and lean, the Earl of Greyhame, short and bacon-faced, and the Marquis of Tennesborne, who spoke with affected syllables so as to make himself sound more important than he was.

He was glad, or rather he should be, for the reprieve of dealing with Mary.

Miss Smith.

Last night he had come unbearably close to an unforgivable breach of control.

He had nearly reached out and put his thumb on her lip. It had looked petal-soft and enticing. And when she said that he was her master...

The way she had looked at him.

Her breath had quickened, her pulse fluttering in her throat.

She had been untouchable on the surface, but he could see, in every line of her body, that she had desired him.

In the way he desired her.

That the game between them had shifted into something else. It had been there the entire time, but her playing the part of submissive governess had dangerously stoked the fire between them.

How could she possibly know? He was not a man of exacting rules, as some men with his tastes were.

He preferred to give commands to a point, and then allow the rawness of the act to overtake him. It was the only time he could find true release.

It was the only time he allowed himself loose from his chains.

And what he enjoyed was for women who were accustomed to such things to give back as good as they got.

He had never, ever done such things with his wife.

He had been courteous and caring towards her always. Because that was what the act was meant to be between a man and wife.

He had accepted that his days of being allowed release like that were over.

He gritted his teeth.

It did not do to have such fantasies about his children's governess, especially not when sitting at the dinner table with Jane's cousin.

'I heard that you have had difficulty keeping governesses in your employ,' said the Earl's wife.

'I have had trouble finding someone qualified,' he said.

Because while he could admit that his children's behaviour was part of the problem, he would not say such a thing in front of these people.

'And the infant,' said the Earl. 'How has he fared with the loss of his mother?'

He felt his muscles tense. 'As babes do. He is not conscious of the loss.'

And they did not ask for the child's name, for which he was relieved.

They did not care. They were here because they wished to keep their ties with him. He knew that. He was a convenient stop on the way to Bath and he was valuable for his wealth and connections. Not because they cared for him or his children. Not because they cared for the babe. Not in the least.

His wife had been the daughter of an earl, and their marriage had been very advantageous to her family as far as connection.

He knew now that the only reason they sought an audience with him was to ensure that they were still in his favour.

He felt pity for Jane then. Had she been nothing more than a symbol to everyone? Had anyone known her?

The thought made his stomach turn sour.

'I see you have a new governess.' This came from Lord Pelham, whose wife sat to his left. And yet West sensed something lascivious beneath those words.

He had seen Mary. It was clear to West from the tone the other man spoke in that he had admired Mary.

Perhaps that is simply what you hear because you cannot fathom a man looking upon her and not feeling attraction, since you are unable to control your own.

'Indeed,' he said, a warning inherent in his tone. 'She arrived here four days ago.'

'She seems quite young.' Again, an observation West felt was tinged with impropriety, though if Lady Pelham noticed she did not seem to give it a care.

'She is a governess, and therefore her age matters not. She might well be a new settee.'

'You never were a warm man,' Blackwater said, laughing. 'But that is why you are so good with your investments, I think.'

'If you wish to talk investments,' Blackwater's wife said, 'then perhaps it is time we quit the table.'

The men adjourned to the parlour after dinner, with the wives collecting in the morning room, where his duchess had often entertained.

Perhaps to gossip about him. About how cold he

was. About how it was not simply a governess he saw as a piece of furniture. That he had seen his wife in the same way, most likely.

Maybe they had known of Jane's unhappiness.

Maybe they knew all the ways he had failed as a husband. Things he did not even know.

Things he would never know.

Because it was too late to ask about them now. Too late to talk about them. Too late to go over all the things left unsaid.

'I am looking for investors,' the Earl said. 'For a new venture that I am hoping to aid. Trade routes.'

'I am very particular about trade,' he said.

'I had heard that you were quite moralistic at times, West.'

'Is it moralistic to care whether or not our fellow men are being sacrificed on the altar of commerce? I thought that was simply humanity.'

'It is the way of the world...'

'It is not the way of *my* world,' he said, knowing that his tone made it clear he would hear no argument. 'I am happy to look into the details of anything that you wish to ask me to invest in, but be warned that if I partake in a particular endeavour I will ensure that it is up to my standards. I tend to cost merchants more. I do make up for it.'

'I didn't know you had such high standards,' said

the Earl. And something glinted in his eye that West found distasteful.

'I do. And if you wish to be in business with me, then that is the way of it.'

'I do not recall my dear cousin having such exacting tastes when she sourced fabrics for her dresses.'

'Whether she knew it or not, I did.'

'Oh, yes. My wife says that you are quite famous for not sharing your mind, rather you are much more interested in issuing edicts.'

Rage burned in his gut. 'I do not need to explain myself. And if my stance bothers you, or perhaps the way I conducted myself in my marriage to your cousin, then you are excused from doing business with me.'

Blackwater scowled. 'Come now, don't be like that. I'm certain that we can find a joint business venture that will benefit us both. It's understandable that you've been blue-devilled these past months.'

They made conversation for a while longer, and West was not certain when he had begun to find it so tedious to even pretend to entertain ideas he didn't care about. Perhaps, as Blackwater said, he was blue-devilled. Perhaps his ability to bear this sort of thing had died with Jane. She had always been gracious, even to those who didn't deserve it.

It was another thing he'd been drawn to in her. She was so warm, even when those around her were cold.

Even when he was cold.

The men slowly filtered out of the parlour and he went to pour himself a brandy. He looked at the clock. It was five minutes until the time when he would have met Mary. Miss Smith.

He poured himself a measure of amber liquid.

God in heaven, but she made his blood run hot.

He could not, he had just tested this, manufacture interest or concern where he did not possess it. And he could not prevent his all-consuming obsession with her.

West put the brandy down and found himself walking out of the parlour towards his study. Perhaps he might find her there.

Or, at the very least, he would find her note.

He moved close to the study door and heard the sound of voices, one male, the other a woman's. Low and angry.

Mary.

He pushed the door open to find Pelham had her backed up against a bookcase. He moved forward, rage propelling him, when he saw Mary pull a knife out of her corset and hold the blade up against the edge of the man's throat. 'I asked you kindly to leave.'

He froze, as did Pelham, who turned to look at him, his whole body stiff.

'Do you see this?' Pelham asked. 'Do you see...? Tell her to stop.'

'What were you doing, Pelham?'

'It's nothing. A bit of light conversation that she…' He coughed. 'Lower your weapon.'

Mary's lip twisted upward. 'Step away from me.'

She held the knife out, her expression immovable, and Pelham removed himself, taking two steps back and nearly tripping over his feet as he did.

'God's teeth, keep that bitch away from me.'

West strode forward and grabbed the man by the collar. 'Leave my house,' he growled, before releasing him, causing him to stumble again, and he was damned lucky West hadn't chosen to land a facer on him.

'Your Grace…' Mary said.

'Not you,' he said. 'Pelham, you will leave my house now. If you are quick about it I will not offer an explanation to your travelling companions. But if you tarry I will make sure to announce to all of them that my governess had to pry you away from her at knifepoint.' There was no legal recourse for such a thing, of course. Mary was the one likely to be arrested and charged.

He had walked in on what many would call nothing more than a miscommunication.

But he knew. He knew that if he had not been there…

No. Mary had saved herself.

He had, perhaps, saved Pelham.

'We thought we needed you,' said Pelham. 'But no one will be doing business with you. You will do yourself out of money with your moral code, West. And how superior will you feel to the rest of us when you have your elevated title, and not a penny to spend?'

'I will sleep better than I would if I exploited children, women, for my own pleasure. My own game. I refuse to do that, for all the wealth on earth. And I will sleep just fine with those standards, thank you.' He rang his bell and his butler, Barrows appeared. 'Barrows, please escort Lord and Lady Pelham out of the house. You may give them a carriage to see him safely back to London.'

'Yes, Your Grace,' he said.

Without argument or a demand for an explanation, which was why he valued Barrows like he did. He gestured to the door, and Pelham looked at him with rage in his eyes.

'Do not test me,' West said, keeping his gaze level on Pelham's. 'If you were to vanish from my home tonight I would tell all who asked that you had disappeared into the night and I had no clue where you had gone. No one would bother to dig in the garden for you.'

His words rested heavy in the room, resonant and dark. True.

He had seen death. It would mean nothing to him to end the life of a man who would harm a woman.

'Is that a threat, West?' Pelham asked.

'Threats are for men who answer to a higher power. I answer to none but myself. Leave, before I decide it is less work to dismember you than procure you a carriage.'

Violence flooded his veins. He was his father's son, and he felt no guilt at the thought of meting out that kind of justice in this circumstance. He could discern between the desire to destroy an abusive man and the indiscriminate pain men like his father meted out.

He turned to Mary, who was standing there, her arms stretched tight at her sides, the knife gripped in her fist, her hold so intense her knuckles had turned white.

His instinct was to touch her.

He would not. Not after Pelham had been so close to her, touching her when she did not wish him to.

'Are you hurt?' he asked.

She shook her head, but did not lower the knife.

'You are safe,' he said.

She took a shaking breath, and then tucked the knife back into her corset. Exactly where it went, and how it was fitted, he couldn't say for sure.

'Do you always travel with a weapon?'

'As I said to you on the first day—' her voice was shaking, but was still strong '—I am a woman in the world, and I am not ignorant of the workings of it. You cannot be. Not when you are left on your own the way that I have been.'

'Mary,' he said.

'Miss Smith. Please. I do not believe that we are on such familiar terms, Your Grace.'

She straightened up tall, craning her neck, tilting her chin upward.

'You are safe,' he repeated.

'Am I? I have not had occasion to use a knife on a man in quite some time. And certainly never while in a household position.'

'I can only apologise. I did not know the manner of man he was. I will ensure that no one else will be surprised by him. You and I both know there would be no effect going to the authorities, but I will do so if it makes you feel secure.'

She shook her head. 'No. It will do nothing. What happened? Nothing. He made an advance towards me. I rebuffed him.'

'In my own household. One of my staff. It is unconscionable, even my wife's cousin will think so, and he is not a man of great principle.'

'You are angry,' she said. 'Because you see me as your property, and disrespect shown to me is disrespect shown to you. Is that not so?'

He pushed his fingers through his hair, to keep himself from drawing near to her. 'I am angry because you were nearly hurt. I am angry because of what would've happened if I did not enter this room.'

'I would've cut his throat without hesitation. On that, I hope we're clear. I did not need you to save me from him. Though I thank you for saving me from the gallows, because that is likely where that would've ended.'

She meant it. He could see it in her eyes. The conviction there.

'Who are you, Miss Mary Smith?'

She shook her head. 'I am no one of consequence. I am only a woman trying to live. My past doesn't matter. It means nothing to me. And it should be nothing to you.'

'There is a reason you carry that knife.'

'Because it is so much better to have the knife and not need it, than to need it and wish you had it.'

'A good philosophy. I cannot argue with you.'

'When you press me about my past, you are no different than him. Men who think that they are owed something they are not. I have said that I don't wish to speak about Scotland. That it doesn't matter, and yet you persist.'

'It is not the same, with my apologies. It is not the same. You are caring for my children, and if there are things in your past that I need to know about I feel entitled to ask them.'

'After this many days you still do not trust me?'

He lifted his brow, looking pointedly at the place she had just put the knife.

'It is to defend myself. As you could see.'

'In many ways it gives me even more confidence in you.'

She nodded once. 'I would defend your children as well.'

'I gather that.'

He moved closer to her, and she shrank just slightly. 'West...'

Her use of his name, even if not his Christian name, but the familiar name by which his friends knew him, stopped him.

'I would never hurt you,' he said.

She nodded slowly. 'I know that. You are not the kind of man who derives pleasure from the fear of others.'

He shook his head. 'No. I am not.'

His father had been that man. He had loved to hold them all hostage with his wild rages. With his capricious moods. They had all had front row seats to his tumultuous love affairs, and his mother had been torn asunder by them.

It was the pain that his father had seemed to enjoy the most. A true sadist.

And while there were elements of sexual sadism that West himself took some enjoyment in, only when it was mutually desired. One should never subject another human being to that which they did not joyfully agree to.

It was not enough for him to have simple, grudging compliance. Even when he bought women he insisted upon women who shared his tastes. Not women who simply endured.

A man like his father, a man like Pelham, they were…

'If I had my way men like that would hang. Every one of them. Because what you and I both know to be true is that they don't change. It is not a moment. It is not one instance in a study. It is their way of looking at the world. It is the enjoyment they get from it. It is heedless and reckless and selfish. And we would all be better off if they did not draw breath.'

A smile touched her lips. 'It pleases me to hear you say that.'

It was a moment where they connected. A moment where they understood each other. Wholeheartedly.

'I will accompany you to your room. With the other guests in the house, I will not leave you to make your way alone.'

She hesitated. 'Thank you.'

Then she stopped at his desk and picked up a folded piece of paper. 'I was here to deliver this.'

'I had come to retrieve it.'

He took the letter from her hands, and their fingertips brushed.

He felt a lick of flame down low in his gut, and mentally cursed himself as shameless for feeling that heat when she had only just been harassed.

'You can tell me yourself, while we walk to your room.'

'Very well. Today was better. Tomorrow I plan on taking them out. We will go to the garden and have our tea there. I am working with them on identifying different plants. A bit of botany. To go with their science.'

'The previous governesses did not teach science.'

'I wish for them to have a broad range of knowledge. Anything that I know, they ought to know.'

'Such as how to stow knives on their person and defend themselves if the need arises?'

'Would that be a bad thing?'

'No.'

He realised then that he would be pleased if his own daughter could wield a knife in such a way as to protect herself.

'I would not refuse my children having such an education.'

'We shall see.'

They walked up the stairs and down the long corridor. 'True to your word, you have not offered me any advice.'

'I...'

And then suddenly, there in the darkness, she began to tremble.

'Mary?'

She sagged against the wall and he moved forward without a thought, gripping her arms and holding her there, studying her. She was soft. But she was shaking, and that took precedence to his revelation over her softness.

He held her firm and fast, just trying to be steady. It was the one thing he knew how to be. Constant.

He had resisted touching her for his own sake. He did so now for hers.

He did not know how to talk to somebody about their feelings. He did not know how to talk about his own. He did not know how to feel his own.

But he could be there. He could hold fast. It was the only way he knew to be. And so he held her there while she shook.

'I'm sorry,' he said, his voice rough. 'I am sorry that you have had occasion to feel unsafe in my household.'

And there was no room for games now, for needling her.

He did not wish to tear down the walls, not now. Because he felt as if he was seeing behind them in this moment, and it made him feel undone. He liked her strong. He liked her wilful and fighting.

He did not wish to see her shaken.

'I am… I am not afraid of him. Of any man. I did

everything I hoped I might do when cornered. I could have saved myself. What I fear is… I would have killed him. I would have.'

'You would've been right to do so.'

She shook her head. 'No. No, I…'

'You did not advance upon him. You did not create the problem. Do not feel guilt over it now.'

'I am terrified at what I came so close to. And I am grateful that I did not have to. And also filled with regret that the man still walks the earth.'

And he understood. She didn't want to have to be the one to cut his throat, but thinking of Pelham, as he was, out in the world, was a disturbing thought.

'He will think twice. He will think twice before he ever treats a woman this way again. Because of you. He will never be entirely certain that a woman does not have a knife in her corset.'

'Yes. That is true.'

He was still holding her, and it was a strange sort of revelation.

Jane had never gone to him for comfort. They simply hadn't had that sort of relationship. It had been companionable. For a long time. And he had loved her. But she had not gone to him when she was in an emotional state.

She had never leaned against him like this.

And suddenly it was as if Mary realised that she

was allowing him to hold her, and she moved away from him. 'Thank you again, Your Grace.'

She turned away from him and began to walk towards her room. 'I can find my way from here.'

He nodded, and watched as she disappeared into her chamber.

And he was left with a raw heart, his palms burning.

He decided that he would be sending some well-placed letters, to destroy all of that bastard's business arrangements.

Because he could not send a man to the gallows. But he would hang him financially, socially.

It was in his power to do so.

He was a duke.

And the man would not forget it.

Chapter Seven

She was fuzzy-headed and distracted after everything that had happened last night...

That man would have raped her.

He had seen her and decided he was entitled to her body. He'd thought he had the right to her because she was a woman, and because she was not a lady.

But she had not been a girl. A thirteen-year-old with no idea of what the man meant to do, and no means to protect herself. She had practised with that knife. Practised taking it from her bodice and holding it, just like that. Either at a man's throat, or at his cock.

She had prepared, and that preparation had meant she'd been able to protect herself and she was...

She was not reduced. She had thought she might be. That she would collapse, having been faced with a shade of her past pain again. But she was not the same and she'd proven that. It was almost intoxicating. She'd had the strength to kill him if she'd needed it and by God she would have. She'd have faced the gallows with pride.

But West had been there. Afterwards, she had fallen apart, and he had held her.

His strength had been used to comfort.

It was a revelation. One she had not asked for. One she did not *wish* for.

But this strange feeling of power that now suffused her was wrapping itself around her appreciation for his strength. Almost as if her own strength made it acceptable to enjoy his.

She would see him again tonight.

In fact, she could think of nothing else.

She would see him again. Tonight. After he had put his hands on her, held her fast while she had trembled. She'd been strong until she was safe, and then he had been there.

No one had ever been there for her before.

A man's hands on her had never been comforting.

They had never been…compelling.

'Let us move on to Latin,' she said, her voice sterner than she intended as she thought of how tight his grip had been.

My master.

What would it be like? To have him in charge of her care, as he was of all of the estate and everyone in it…

Heaven save her.

By the time the day ended, she walked into his

study with grit and determination as her guide. She would face him, and she would not betray that she was affected by him.

He was standing already.

'Are you all right?'

She nodded once. 'Just fine.'

'I want you to know, I decided to ruin him.'

She blinked. 'What...?'

'His business relationships will be in tatters after the letters I have written. He will not find it easy to earn money, not in England, not any more. The endeavours they were engaged in were not, in my opinion, of sound moral value anyway. But I took it upon myself to ensure that his partnerships would cease to exist.'

'You are every bit as ruthless as I am, aren't you?'

'Yes. But not of necessity. Because I am a duke, and it is my right.'

She had wondered what it would be like to have strength and power wielded in her favour, and this was it. This, right here.

She did not quite know what to make of it.

She still thought he was likely more angry that his home had been disrespected than anything else. But it was certainly more protection than had ever been offered her before.

'Thank you,' she said. 'However—' she took a

breath '—we should keep to our business. Which is, of course, the children.'

It was easier to talk about the children. Safer. Better.

'They enjoyed seeing the plants today.'

'And you were able to continue with your position?'

'I'm not… I'm not fragile, Your Grace, whatever you think of me because of what you witnessed last night. Remember the knife, and not the trembling. And, if you must, remember that I shook not from fear of him, but fear over the very real truth that he would have made a murderer of me.'

'I will never forget either.'

'You are more shocked by what occurred than I am. I do not ever give men the benefit of any sort of doubt. I am vigilant. Always.'

And that was the closest she would ever get to speaking of the past with him.

'Shock is not the appropriate word. I am angry. I am a man who prides himself, above all things, on his ability to stay focused. When I must work, I work. If I feel anger, I go and I box. I ride my horse. I do not sit and stew in it while I am supposed to work, and yet today I find that I have. I am preoccupied by my desire to ruin him. And that is not how I am.'

'You are not a man of vengeance?'

'I am not a man of distraction. I am all for vengeance when it fits neatly into my day.'

She could not tell if he was teasing. She did not think he was.

'Why do you care so much?' she asked. The question was so small and needy, and she despised it, but she needed to ask it.

No one had ever held her like he had. She had been distant from his body, but his grip had been tight. And it had been unlike anything else. She wanted to keep her mask in place. She wanted to stay unaffected.

She was not unaffected and right in this moment she simply didn't have the strength to be the governess.

She was Mary.

And he had held her.

His eyes met hers. 'Did you not tell me, I am your master? You are mine.' Her heart was pounding in her ears, and she was trembling, but not in the same manner as last night. 'Part of this household.'

She let out a breath that she had indrawn.

'Your responsibility,' she said.

'Yes,' he confirmed.

She was not his, nor should she want him to make such a statement. And yet for a moment all of her had been held captive by those words. By her longing.

If she belonged to him she could rest. Finally.

If she belonged to him he would protect her, and yes, she was pleased that she had discovered she could protect herself, but the very idea that someone else might also protect her, and not in a distant way, but a personal way…it ignited a need in her that terrified her.

But this was not personal.

It was how he would feel for anyone in his house.

'I am sorry to have taken so much of your time.'

His expression shifted, going stern. 'You were not the cause of this. He was.'

She hadn't realised how good it might feel to hear something like that. She had been blamed. Condemned. Made to fear for her life.

With ease, West…

Why had she called him that last night?

Why was she thinking of him that way?

With ease he had accepted that she was the one who'd been wronged. He believed her, and not the man who had tried to attack her.

She might not be his in a personal sense, but she did have that.

'Thank you. I… I will go to bed now. Today was quite tiring.'

He nodded. 'Of course.'

She wanted to thank him. She wanted to move to him and…she wanted him to touch her again, but instead she drew back.

'Goodnight,' she said, and it sounded intimate somehow.

He said nothing, he only regarded her with those stern blue eyes, and she moved from the room, closing the door firmly behind her. She leaned against it for a moment, trying to catch her breath, trying to find her balance again.

She could feel the impression of his touch lingering still. He had balanced her, and yet left her feeling storm-tossed all at once.

She pushed herself away from the door and walked through to the entrance of the house. It was so vast.

For some reason she felt compelled to move quickly beneath the opulent chandelier, dark now due to the late hour, as if the whole thing might come crashing down on her if she weren't careful.

As if everything that protected her was coming undone.

It made no sense why she should feel that way. She had protected herself from that…from that predator of a man.

It is not the predator you worry about.

No. Indeed.

She did not worry about protecting herself from the Duke. She worried about what she…what she might do. Not he.

She walked up the stairs, and down the corridor. And, like the other night, heard the babe wailing. She stopped and waited. Waited for that wet nurse to appear.

She didn't come. And the babe continued to cry, his screams becoming more and more pathetic.

She took a sharp breath, and she had that feeling again. Like the whole ceiling might collapse upon her. Like everything was crumbling.

She did not know why. But it was as if she couldn't find her defences.

And this child had none.

That hit her with more force than the ceiling ever could have.

She was a woman. A woman of two and twenty years who had just pulled a knife on a man who had frightened her. She felt bruised and battered, yes. But she had defences.

This child did not.

This child with no name.

The wet nurse wasn't coming. This child could not save himself.

He was dependent, and surrounded by people who could not get past their own wounds in order to see to him.

Galvanised, she stepped forward, pushing open the door to the nursery.

It was empty, other than the bairn.

She crossed the room slowly and looked down into the crib.

The child was screeching, kicking impotent fists and feet into the air.

She did not know how to pick a child up out of

the cradle. So she stood there, uselessly. Feeling the weight of her past folding in on her.

And she pushed it back. She didn't want to remember this.

You are not English.

From the moment she had set foot in this house it was as if her past was closer than ever before.

It was as if him uncovering that truth had brought it up to the surface.

And then there was Pelham. The way he had cornered her, the way that it had forced her to think about her attack at thirteen. The way she had changed the outcome.

It was not all wounding. Some of it was, in fact, healing, but it was all right bear all the shame, and deeply disconcerting in its way.

She reached out and put her fingertips against the babe's belly.

He hiccupped, and then stilled.

She drew her hand away, anxiety lancing her. And then she put her hand back, resting it more firmly on his stomach, rubbing him back and forth like she might a kitten.

'It's all right,' she said soothingly. 'Food will be here soon.'

It had better be.

The babe quieted and a moment later the door creaked open. And there she was. The wet nurse.

'Where have you been?' Mary asked, not pausing to think about the fact that she was likely stepping out of bounds by lecturing another member of the household.

'Not your concern, miss high-and-mighty,' said the woman.

'It is my concern. Because this is the second time the babe has been in distress and you have not been here. You are meant to be here.'

'Am I not allowed to use the necessary?'

'If that is what you were doing. I don't believe that it is.'

'It isn't your job to tell me how to do mine. It is not your concern.'

'The children are my concern.'

The woman looked through the darkness at her. 'Are you shagging him?'

She was taken aback by the crude question, but she knew immediately who the woman meant. Unbidden, it created images in her mind. His strong body over hers. And never in her life had that image infused her with anything but revulsion, and yet in this moment… revulsion was not what she felt.

She pushed it aside, allowing anger to guide her.

She would not be cowed by this, not this woman.

'If I was *shagging him*,' she said, 'I would still see to my responsibilities. Whatever you're off doing is preventing you from doing yours, and that is the issue.

I don't care whose bed you occupy, but I do care if it keeps you from being where you were meant to be.'

'It isn't going to kill the child to wait a moment to be fed.'

But the cries killed her. Slowly and by inches, and she could not bear it.

'See to him,' she said.

The woman approached the cradle and took the babe out, releasing her breast and latching him on easily. 'There. You can go now.'

Mary gave the woman a long look as she walked out of the room, her heart beating painfully.

Are you shagging him?

She blinked back stinging moisture from her eyes, and she could not say why all of this felt so raw. So uncontrolled. Only that it did.

She went to her bedroom and closed the door firmly behind her.

Between Pelham and the Duke and the babe, the wet nurse, she felt like pieces of all her defences were being torn away. Revealing truths.

She was stronger than she had feared she might be, but she was also more susceptible to other things that she had not yet imagined.

She was determined that she would weather this. She was determined to find her footing again.

Chapter Eight

The next day with the children, she continued to think about the bairn.

How pitiful he had been. How guilty she felt that he did not have a consistent champion.

The wet nurse was here to care for him, to feed him, but it was her job, and she was not in any way caring for whether or not he was... Nurtured.

Having had a childhood with parents who had not seen to the care and keeping of their brood, she felt especially sensitive to that.

Or perhaps it just made her think of her son.

He isn't your son. Not really. He was born of your body, but you never even held him.

No. She hadn't.

She hadn't, and it was an ache that she did not think she would ever truly banish from her soul.

'Should you not like your brother to join us in the nursery some time?' she asked Michael and Elizabeth impulsively, without even thinking about it.

She wasn't certain that she wanted him to join them in the nursery, and yet she was concerned now about his isolation.

'No,' said Elizabeth.

'Why not?'

'He's an infant,' said Michael. 'He cannot be in here. It is a classroom.'

'It is a place for children.'

'No,' Elizabeth said, shaking her head. 'We don't want him. He killed our mother.'

Her words stabbed Mary in the chest, and Mary tried, she tried to the best of her ability, to find that stoic governess within. 'Childbirth killed your mother,' she said. 'But the child was only as helpless as she was. She was his mother too.'

Flashes came into her mind, of her own experience. Of nearly dying.

'How?' Elizabeth asked.

'Well… Childbirth is extremely fraught. It can be dangerous. It is a medical event.'

'I don't understand,' said Elizabeth, looking red-faced and furious.

'There are books. Science books. And it can help explain.'

She knew that people did not often teach children these things. But their mother had died this way. And would that not help them to understand? She had needed to understand. She had given birth without having any idea of what was to happen to her. She had been raped, having no idea how a child was made, or that men did such things to women.

The world was a brutal place, and it did not care whether or not women or children were educated in the realities of it.

And she knew that the Duke might be upset if he found out she taught his children such things, but she would defend her reasoning.

The thought of Elizabeth going into a marriage with absolutely no knowledge whatsoever... It filled her with terror.

And no, she did not need to know everything that passed between men and women just yet, but should she not know these simple things? The very basic truths of biology? Would it not arm her?

It wounded her, the way that girls were sent into the marriage bed with no knowledge at all.

Perhaps they were not being held down in the field. But it would be confusing and frightening, and far too close to what Mary herself had experienced.

'I promise we will make it part of your lesson. But while this is the way that children come into the world, it is a dangerous thing. And many women die doing it.'

Elizabeth looked frightened. 'That doesn't make any sense.'

'Many women don't die. It is not something that you should have to worry about, but the worst happened in your lives, so of course you will. It is a terrible thing to have to grow up before you are meant to. And I think, with this loss, you have had to.'

'I still don't want to see the babe,' she said.

'Just remember,' she said. 'He lost his mother too. He has you. He has your father. But that's all. Perhaps you could spare him a bit of pity.'

'No,' Michael said, standing and furiously kicking over a chair. 'He killed her. He's why she's dead. I hate him.'

And, without thinking, Mary dropped down to her knees and pulled Michael into a fierce hug. 'Michael,' she said. 'It's all right.' Because it was. To be furious, to be angry. To rail against the universe. She was well acquainted with that need.

How she had hated the bairn that grew inside of her. She had been disgusted by him when he had been born. And when he was quiet for a moment she had thought perhaps her worries had ended.

She was well acquainted with how dark your thoughts could become when you were grieving and wounded and twisted up in your soul.

And even though she wanted now to offer some protection to the child, she understood that Michael and Elizabeth needed to drain the poison from within them by giving voice to these terrible, awful feelings inside of them. Maybe when she taught them about childbirth, they would be able to understand. Hold it all at a distance and comprehend that these were the sorts of things that happened, and it was not done with intent. It had taken that kind of knowledge for her to be able to put her own memories at a distance. To be able to examine them dispassionately. But, until then, sometimes rage was what saw you through.

But she held him, because no one had held her. She held him, because his mother was gone, and she wondered if anyone had held him since.

She was not a woman given to these sorts of displays. She did not foster emotional closeness with her charges.

But it was the same realisation she had had about the babe last night. Someone had to be there like this.

Someone had to care.

Their father…

He was lost in whatever his own grief was wringing from him, and he could not be what they needed.

It made her ache.

This sort of fractured pain in this family.

'You don't know anything,' he said, pushing her.

And she let him.

What could she say? That she did. That she had grown up with nothing and no one and knew what it was like to be lonely. That she knew how it was to be in pain and to have no one to reach out to.

That would mean exposing herself. And she did not wish to do that.

'We do not have to bring the babe in here,' she said. 'I'm sorry.'

They both looked at her, shocked at her apology. 'I'm sorry for him too. My feelings have not changed. But I am sorry that it hurts you so.'

If they could see that that at least was revolutionary. That she offered them recognition of their feelings.

It was all she could do. Because to say anything more would expose herself, and she couldn't bear it. Not after the past few days had left her scraped raw.

She was exhausted again by the end of the day, and by the time she had to go and face the Duke in his study she was not sure how she would bear standing beneath that imperious blue gaze again. He saw into her, and she could not see into him. She had no idea what he felt. What he cared about.

He cared about protecting the people in his household, that was true. But he did not seem to know how to connect with them. Did he love them? Did he even love his children? Since that first day she had not seen him interact with them. He asked for a distant report, and that was all. She had told him that she would make no more suggestions, and yet she did not think that could go on.

They were drowning on land, without their father to reach out and save them.

He spoke of the Duchess as if she had been a warm and loving mother, and she wondered if the Duke had been as well, but the Duchess had taken the warmth in this house with her. Perhaps it had only ever been her.

Perhaps he had treated her just the same as he did his children. Perhaps they had been the family, they had been the love, and now it was gone from them.

All of it seemed tragic.

She walked in without thinking to knock.

She realised her mistake when his head jerked up.

'I'm sorry,' she said.

'I was expecting you,' he replied.

'It was inappropriate of me to enter without knocking.'

He ignored her words, and instead subjected her to that brutal, wordless appraisal of his. 'You do not look well.'

She swallowed hard. 'It has been a difficult day. I will be very honest with you. It has been difficult.'

He made her feel both discomfited and deeply vulnerable. She had, yet again, the deep need to move closer to him and keep her distance all at the same time.

Perhaps that was the issue with the man himself. He seemed like a well of intensity. And yet there was a wall up around him so high, she did not know if anyone had ever scaled it.

Are you so different?

Yes. They were different.

He was a man. He was a Duke. He had nothing

to protect himself from. She, on the other hand, had erected her defences out of sheer desperation. Necessity. She was not able to simply live because she would be torn asunder if she did.

If she did not protect herself, nobody would.

All the world protected a duke.

It was different.

He had no right to this.

It wasn't fair. Here she was, caught up in the burning flames of all this, and there he sat.

'Michael had another very difficult day.'

'I will speak to him.'

She was taken aback. 'You will?'

'He is not to treat you with disrespect.'

'I do not wish for Michael to be punished. He is a little boy and he has experienced a great loss…'

'It is no excuse for treating his governess poorly.'

'I do not care for how he treats me. I am an adult, and I can bear it. The problem is his pain. If you wish to speak to him, Your Grace, then do so, but not to punish him. He does not deserve that. He needs someone to come alongside him and offer comfort.'

'I will consider it.'

She bit her tongue. He would consider offering his son comfort.

Was he, in fact, entirely made of ice?

He stared at her, and she felt a growing heat in her

stomach that made a mockery of what she had just thought.

'I…'

'Will that be all?'

She steeled herself, prepared now to broach the topic of the babe.

'No. That is not all.'

'What, then?'

'There is the matter of the wet nurse. I believe that she is being lax in her duties.'

'In what sense?'

'I think she may be having a dalliance with someone else in the household.'

'What evidence have you of that?'

'Twice now I have heard the babe crying, and there was no one in his room. I have a concern that she is not wedded to her responsibilities as she should be.'

'And you are certain she is away because she is engaging in an affair?'

'No. It is only a feeling that I have.'

'I will have Mrs Brown speak to her.'

'Thank you, Your Grace.'

'Anything else?'

She closed her eyes.

'Your Grace,' she said. 'I do just have a question about the babe. Does he truly not have a name? Only there are times when…'

'No,' he said.

That poor child. He was such a pitiable creature. No name, and not even a hint of regret or warmth when his father spoke of him.

'It does not seem...'

'It is not your concern.'

'Sometimes, Your Grace, the child has come close to being my concern, and upon my arrival Mrs Brown and I spoke about what was to be done if ever the wet nurse is indisposed, or not available when need be. It was made quite clear to me that it would fall beneath my area of work, and I take that seriously.'

'The child does not have a name.'

And he did not go to see the child either.

She felt immense pain in that moment.

She'd avoided the babe, and his own father did as well.

His mother was dead.

The children hated him.

There was tragedy everywhere. In every brick of this house. But life, in her experience, was a great tragedy. No one chose these things. They were not pebbles children collected on a beach. They had been given these burdens to bear, all of them.

These things were inescapable. And ignoring the babe was hardly going to erase the pain in her past.

'I thought we had agreed that you were to make no more suggestions to me.'

It was easy to be angry at him, but he had lost his

wife. It was easy to be angry when she felt like she was bleeding whenever she thought of their loss. It was easy to believe he was a rock wall and nothing more.

She knew it wasn't true. It couldn't be.

Because of how he'd held her.

Because of how he'd wanted to protect her.

'I'm not making a suggestion,' she said. 'I'm simply trying to clarify what I am certain is a painful and irregular situation.'

'I'm not preventing you from having more to do with the child if you wish.'

'He should be christened.'

'There will be a time,' he said, his voice rough. 'But it is not now.'

She had been a mother unable to hold her child. For so many reasons, and this child's mother was much the same. She felt… She was tired of feeling weak. What had happened last night had not necessarily made her feel weak. If anything, it had proven to her how much she had changed. Fear might have shaped her these last years, but at least it had been with purpose. It had accomplished something. It had made her stronger.

And so… Perhaps she needed to be stronger than her grief from all those years ago because they could not be stronger than their grief from these months.

'Your Grace,' she said. 'I…'

'On the subject of the infant we have nothing to say to one another.'

He was icy then.

She looked at him, her brow knit together. She felt…
Drawn to him. Compelled. Two nights ago, when she
had fallen apart, he had held her together.

She wanted to do the same for him. To hold him
steady so he could feel.

So he could take a full breath, for how could he?
He was protected by that wall, but he was trapped by
it too.

Her heart hurt so badly it was difficult not to cry
out with the pain.

Before she realised what she was doing, she had
crossed the space. She came to stand before his desk,
the pull inside of her too great to bear.

He looked up at her, the blue of his eyes the only
real thing.

She rounded the side of his desk and moved even
closer to him. No protection now, for that desk had
been a barrier and it was not any more.

Without pausing to think, she lowered herself before
him. As she had done earlier for Michael. She looked
up, lifted her trembling hand to place it on his cheek.

It was rough with stubble from the day, and hot.
So very hot. She slowly moved her thumb back, then
forward, as she had done when comforting the babe.
But immediately she was seized by a sensation that
was not maternal in any fashion.

The desire to rest her head on his lap, to have him cradle her head...

She looked down and noticed his hands, large and battered, resting on his thighs, and her heart pounded, painfully.

It served as a jolt back to reality. She scrambled back, getting to her feet.

'Forgive me.'

'Mary...'

'Miss Smith,' she said, shaking her head. 'It is Miss Smith. And I am sorry. It's only that... You're in pain and... But it is not my pain. It is not my pain to bear.'

She turned and practically fled the study.

It was all of these things. She was distracted. She was overwrought.

These feelings for him had been building this past week, and she had been in control of it. She had been able to deal with it, until last night. When she had gone into the babe's room and wept along with him. It was... It was unbearable sometimes, what the world did to you.

And she was confusing him again with one of her charges. He was not.

She needed to keep her distance from him.

She needed to keep herself from falling to pieces. And she did not know how to do that. Because it was not that man in the study last night who had undone her. It was the care that he had shown her after.

It was the way that she, even with fresh reminders of the perfidy of men, wished to lean into him, not pull away from him.

She had to remember why she was here. It was the children. It was…

Stability? And where is that? Every day here has been painful and confusing. There is nothing stable here. Perhaps you should leave.

No. She was not going to leave. Because that would be admitting defeat.

She would not do that. She was stronger than this. Stronger than errant feelings that meant nothing. Absolutely nothing.

Tomorrow, she would take the children out for more botany. She would do her job. She would be the person that she had chosen to be.

She did not allow men to decide. All that mattered was what she chose. She was in control.

She had to remember that.

Chapter Nine

She and Mrs Brown had worked out a system for dealing with the absent wet nurse, and the older woman had made it clear she was looking for a replacement so they could release the current girl from her position.

And, until today, the responsibility of the child had yet to fall to Mary.

But as she was readying to move to the next lesson with the children, she could hear the babe begin to cry.

And she was back in Scotland. Eight years ago.

She was exhausted, the life draining from her, as she looked up at the midwife who held a tiny, silent babe in her arms.

Mary had never been so tired in her life. Her whole body was like broken glass. Her heart, and outward. The indignity of all she had suffered, all she had not asked to suffer, from when she had first been forced to the ground by the man who had harmed her, to carrying the babe, and then nature wrenching the child from her body in such a grotesque and terrifying way, and she…a child who had no knowledge of any of it.

Then the babe gave a cry, and Penny took him. A flurry of movement happened around her, words that began to grow frayed at the edges until she could no longer hear. Until she was cold and her vision began to go dark…

Michael and Elizabeth's mother had died giving birth.

Mary was brought back to the present, to the child before her.

She had nearly lost her life, she understood that now. She had not fully understood then, for she had understood nothing that had happened to her.

She had made a study of it since. In an attempt to turn the bloody horror of that day into something scientific in nature, something she could comprehend.

Once she had learned to read, she had consumed information as if it were nourishment and she was a starving child. In many ways, she was.

In the library at school there were scientific texts on the highest shelves which had explained procreation between men and women, and childbirth. She had read each one five times. Piecing together the violence of what had happened to her that afternoon in the village with her quickening, and the birth after.

She had not understood any of it at the time.

Giving herself the chance to understand in very

basic ways what had happened, and why, had given her the ability to hold it at a distance, examine it.

But the crying baby made her think of her son.

No. That baby was not her son.

Her son was happy. He was well cared for. He would be the next leader of Clan McKenzie. He was loved fiercely by the parents who had taken him in as their own.

Though she knew Penny had intended to tell him, when the time was right, that another woman had given birth to him...

Those hours she'd spent giving birth to him did not make a lifetime.

He was not her son, not truly. And yet he was a child born of her body, and so he would never not have a tie to her. A connection.

It would never be that easy.

And she may never be able to think of him as anything other than her son. For there was no other word to express what she felt.

She was grateful. Grateful that he had gone on to have the life he did. Grateful that he had not lived with her beneath the stigma. And grateful to herself for choosing to leave. Because she could not have imagined staying and watching him, trying to observe a careful distance and yet never being able to have him. Any more than she could fathom attempting to be his mother at thirteen years old.

She had discussed this with Mrs Brown now that they were sharing responsibility of the child in this time when there was no one else, and she had been instructed on how to give the child a bubby pot—a white ceramic pot with a tea towel placed over the spout to slow the flow of milk.

And yet she did not feel prepared.

She looked at the children, who were growing visibly uncomfortable the longer the baby cried. She could feel her own stomach knotting up tighter and tighter as she fought to catch her breath.

'I will fetch your brother. I'll only be a moment.'

She went from the nursery into the babe's room, her heart pounding hard.

There was something so strange about the moment. As if she had one foot here, and one foot back in time. Back in Scotland.

He was wretched. Small and red-faced, and badly in need of a caregiver.

She had not held her own child. At first she'd been too weak to do so. She had bled so much the strength had drained from her body and it had taken time for her to be able to even lift her hand.

But then whenever she'd looked at the child she'd been overcome. By rage. By sorrow.

And the Laird's wife had held the babe and it had seemed…right.

In all the time since, Mary had never held an infant.

She had never been a governess for a family that had a babe, and it had not been deliberate. Truthfully, with eight years between herself and that moment, she had not thought that it would affect her quite so deeply.

She hadn't picked him up the other night when she'd seen him wailing. She hadn't been able to bring herself to do that.

But if she didn't, no one would.

This child was a casualty of all this chaos. The death of his mother. The disinterest of the wet nurse.

The distance of his father.

Her own wretched damage.

He deserved none of it.

She reached down and picked the infant up from the cradle, a deep, crushing sensation overtaking her. Like she had been standing in the rocks by the seashore only to be overtaken by the waves, the force of them pinning her to the rocks.

She pressed his warm body to her breast, and then rang the bell she had been told to use to signal her need of food for the child.

He was fussing still when she carried him back into the children's room.

'Michael, please read the next—'

'We can't concentrate with him squawking,' said Elizabeth.

'He will have food soon,' she said. 'Then he won't squawk.'

Or rather, she hoped not.

She looked down at the tiny babe. He was barely more than a featherweight in her arms.

So small and so fragile.

He made her ache.

'Well, I don't want him in here,' said Elizabeth.

Mary wasn't certain she did either.

'He is your brother,' Mary said.

'He isn't,' she answered.

'I'm sorry,' said Mary. 'It must be difficult. Since the loss of your mother.'

Loss.

The word echoed inside her.

Loss.

She looked down at the pitiful little bundle in her arms.

Loss.

Elizabeth looked at her, hurt shining out from her eyes. 'I don't want to talk about her.'

'Sometimes it's good to talk about things that hurt.'

As though Mary had ever spoken of these things. Of being raped. Of giving birth. Of giving that child away—and gladly—yet still sometimes feeling echoes of disquiet.

She would not change what she had done. It was the only choice she'd had. The only piece of the ordeal that had not been forced upon her.

But that did not mean she didn't experience sadness.

Choosing to let the Laird and his wife raise the child as their own did not mean the past was gone. It only meant she had the chance at a different future.

It did not take away the memories of what had happened, it did not make it so she'd not carried a child in her womb that she had resented—hated—all the months she had carried it, from the moment her mother had found out...

Slut.

Harlot.

If your father finds out you'll be dead.

Hide it.

Then bury it in the woods when the time comes.

'What would you know about this?' Elizabeth asked. 'Is your mother dead?'

She could not find the governess inside her. The tightly protected answer she would have given if she were not beset and overcome by the weight of the babe. By the weight of the past.

In her heart, had she not promised to prepare these children for the world? Elizabeth most of all.

And yet she kept her deepest truths locked away tight. For all the world she looked like a proud, perfectly composed governess. And inside she was Mary. Just Mary. Wounded and small and so bruised that her every breath was painful.

How could she look at this child and lie?

Her mother might be dead. And as she looked at the

hurting little girl she decided the truth was the only thing she had. For this child was raw and in pain, and did she not deserve to know she wasn't alone? That there were others who felt the same?

Her father held himself at a distance, kept his pain hidden.

Did they know he felt their pain?

He did, she had seen it in his eyes last night when she had…

Perhaps her mother had been right about her. What other reason, other than her own propensity towards harlotry, could make her feel as she did about the Duke?

The way she'd felt, kneeling before him…

She knew about men. She did not know about pleasure. But there was something about him that made her want to know more about pleasure.

Even now, she thought of it.

Even now, she wasn't safe from it.

'I don't know,' Mary said finally.

Elizabeth frowned. 'How do you not know?'

'I left home eight years ago. And I have not returned.'

'You've never even asked after your mother?' Michael asked, suddenly very interested in her.

She thought of the last time she'd seen her mother.

'What a trick you pulled off, Mary. Did you spread your legs for the Laird too? Is that why he took the bairn as his own?'

She had been sore then, still bleeding at times, and the very idea of letting a man touch her made her ill.

But her mother had blamed her. No matter that Mary said a man had forced himself on her.

'They only do that when ye make yourself available. They know a whore.'

'No. I have not. My mother was cruel.' She adjusted her hold on the babe. 'Perhaps only because life was cruel to her. When I escaped, that is what I considered it. An escape.'

'Where's your home?' Elizabeth asked this with keen interest.

The Duke already knew. They already knew that she wasn't from here, so why not tell the children?

They thought that she would be run out by this. By their overt hostility to the babe, and to her. She would prove to both of them that she was far sturdier than they gave her credit for.

'I'm from Scotland. The Highlands. A very small village, with a large castle at the centre.'

As she spoke she could feel her accent beginning to change. She could feel her words beginning to take the shape of her homeland.

'It's beautiful there. But life was terribly hard. We had no food often.' The children were watching her with rapt focus now. 'The house we lived in was smaller than this very room. I have twelve brothers and sisters.'

'Where are they?'

Her throat went tight. 'I don't know. I was in the

middle of them. Some grown by the time I left. A couple still in leading strings. But I had to leave.' It was simple. It almost sounded like she had decided one day to go on an adventure. It was how she tried to think of it. How she tried to remember it. 'I wanted to see England. And I wished to go to school. I did not know how to read or write. And when I went to school it was based on the goodwill of my laird. My clan leader.'

'Are they those fierce men that wear dresses?' Elizabeth asked.

'Great kilts. You would not be calling them dresses, not to our men. They are mighty warriors.' Lachlan certainly was. He had sought justice for her, and he had sent her to England. He was a better man than most, and yet knowing a man such as him existed had been like balm on a wound.

'Did you love Scotland?' Michael asked.

'I loved pieces of it.' She thought of the mountains, craggy and green. Of the sky, so big and vast. But also of the desperation. The poverty. She had not tasted such hunger or pain since leaving. 'I longed for something more. When I learned to speak French, and to read and to write, it was as if a magical world opened up to me that I did not think I would ever see. When I teach you, I am trying to teach you that same magic that was taught to me.'

'It doesn't feel like magic. It feels like work.'

'You have always known that you would learn it.

Elizabeth, how fortunate you are to be a girl whose father thinks she ought to read.'

'Well, a lady must be accomplished,' said Elizabeth.

'But you are not a lady, are you? You're a little girl.' Two years younger than herself when she gave birth. And the thought made her throat ache even more.

'I am lady enough.'

'And you can read. And run. And learn French. And yes, some day you will have the concerns of the household, but you do not have them now. What you have now is this chance. To learn everything that you might wish. And I am a great fan of science. And of the natural order of things. We can go for walks around the grounds and I can teach you the names of all the plants. Of all the animals. We can find hedgehogs.'

'I don't like hedgehogs,' said Elizabeth, wrinkling her nose.

'What's not to like about a hedgehog? They are such fearsome creatures. Very bold, for something so tiny. I have always quite fancied them myself, and perhaps seen my likeness in them.'

'That's silly,' said Elizabeth.

'Well, perhaps I'm silly,' she said. 'I am, after all, a girl who came down from the mountains to see what was in another country, far, far away. I am a girl who learned to read when she was thirteen years old.'

'And you're to teach us?' Michael asked.

He seemed shocked that he'd been given over to the care of someone who must be quite stupid.

'Yes. Because it is never too late to learn. But if I can give you one gift, it is the understanding that this knowledge is indeed the most glorious gift. Because I don't live in a mud hut any more, do I?'

Elizabeth sniffed. 'You live in my father's home.'

That made her stomach twist. 'Perhaps. And perhaps you do not understand this, Elizabeth, though it is the way of the world for women. Because you also live in your father's home, and some day you will live in your husband's. But what if you are a woman with no husband? Then you must find an occupation. And with the money from my occupation I could rent my own rooms. Though my occupation requires that I live in residence.'

The babe began to squirm and squall again and, thankfully, Mrs Brown arrived with the bubby pot.

She put the spout to his lips and watched him drink greedily.

He fell asleep after, and she moved the children on to mathematics and tried not to sag with relief when the wet nurse arrived.

She felt dizzy.

She did not take the children outside that day, and she was not entirely certain she'd won them over. But at bedtime they were bathed and put into night clothes, and she instructed them in their prayers.

Even Elizabeth did not have a smart comment to make.

Chapter Ten

He still burned from where she had touched him. It had been the simplest, softest of touches. There had been nothing about it that should have made him think of what it would be like to lay her down in his bed.

Or even better, to pull that demure chemise down, all the way down, and expose her breasts. So that he could look on her in that same position she'd been in. On her knees before him, looking up at him with those glorious emerald eyes.

He had wanted to cup her chin and tell her how good she was. He'd wanted to free his cock from the confines of his breeches and guide her lush lips onto his aching staff.

What he wanted was nothing less than obscene.

For a man and his mistress it might be a pleasurable game. But she was his children's governess.

And it was not a game.

She had sought to comfort him. It had been the simplest and sweetest of gestures. Coming from a woman who in many ways did not seem sweet in the least. He had been beset by illicit images of her all day. Of all the different ways he could have guided that interaction. How he could've buried his fingers in her red hair and pulled hard. Encouraging her to take all of him deep into her mouth.

It had been so many years since a woman had done that for him.

He had loved Jane. He would never have betrayed her, nor would he have asked that of her.

He had been told. He had been told you did not ask such things of your wife.

A gently bred lady was not meant for such things.

He had honoured that lesson. He had believed in it.

He growled and poured himself a drink. He was not in the mood to sit and see to correspondence or books tonight.

He undid the cuffs on his shirt, undid his cravat.

He reached up onto the shelf and took a book down, sat in the armchair by the fireplace.

There was maybe part of him that knew he was tempting something.

This pose was not formal.

But then, she was the one who had breached formality last night. She was the one that had dropped to her knees before him.

He shifted uncomfortably as his member swelled inside of his breeches.

It would not do to be in this state when she arrived to speak of the day.

There was a knock. Sharp.

Yesterday she had simply walked in, and he would be lying if he said he had not enjoyed that familiarity to an extent.

She looked pale and drawn. He would have to be a fool not to see that the days spent in his house had seemingly cost her.

When she had arrived she had been more stalwart.

He blamed Pelham.

Though he knew he could not entirely lay the blame at Pelham's feet. Because he knew, he did know, that the babe, and her concern about him, and then what had passed between them was also bothering her.

He found himself wanting to push her again.

Because last night she had taken him to the edge.

He resented it. Resented that she consumed his thoughts. That he could not sit and try to do work without imagining those luscious lips wrapped around him.

Without imagining pinning her to a wall, wrapping his hand around her throat…

He felt himself growing hard again and cut off that train of thought. Ruthlessly.

'Come in.'

'Mrs Brown is having to seek a new wet nurse.'

'Why have I not been informed of this?'

'Because it is in hand, Your Grace. And I will care for the child until a new wet nurse is found.'

'You will?'

She lifted her chin. 'Yes. It is not ideal. She has found someone who can be here part-time, she has her own children and a husband to care for. And so the search will continue.'

'That girl will receive no references from me.'

'Somehow I don't think she's concerned about that. I had an argument with her, and I think that I may have driven her away.'

'She can be driven away then. It's good riddance as far as I'm concerned.'

'I would agree with you. I do not think that she was committed in the way she ought to have been.'

'Your pay will be increased as long as you are caring for the child.'

She shook her head. 'That is not necessary, Your Grace.'

'It is necessary,' he said. 'You were to care for the babe in emergency events only. And now it falls to you to see to the child in an official capacity.'

'I feel for him. I feel for him because he is alone in this world. And if I can bring a small measure of comfort to him, then I will.'

'Do you like to read?' He gestured to the book in his hand, to the shelves behind him.

'Yes, Your Grace.'

'You are permitted to make use of the library.'

'Thank you, Your Grace.'

He had never hated an honorific more than he did in this moment. Because it made him want what he could not have. And it could be so sweet, if she said it while on her knees...

'You're very welcome.'

'There is something that I must ask you.'

'Which is?'

'I wish to teach the children about procreation.'

He could not have been more shocked had she set a wild stoat free in the study.

His mind was cast back to his own introduction to the topic. Which had included a harlot in his room when he was fifteen. His father had thought it funny. He had felt wildly out of control.

It was one of the first moments when he had realised that he had to seek control at all costs.

And no shock that when he was a man, when he chose his sexual encounters for himself, he ensured his own control.

'And why do you wish to teach them this?'

'Because their mother died in childbirth, and they find it frightening and confusing. Your daughter will enter the ballroom in four short years. It is unfathomably soon, I know. She will be looking for a husband, and should she not have some knowledge to go with that? Your son will likely receive an education. When he is old enough to go away to school, then he will likely find his way with his friends. It is different for boys. It is different for men.'

'That is irregular.'

'It is. I don't believe that it should be. I believe that it should be taught. Clinically and scientifically. That is all I'm asking.'

'Because of the death of their mother you find it to be of particular importance?'

She nodded. 'Yes. My mother had thirteen children.' He frowned. 'And I saw her give birth. It was frightening because I didn't understand what was happening. But once I did understand, I could make sense of it. It is simply part of life. Of the world. What I want, all that I want, is to make the children better prepared. And to help them begin to heal from what has happened. And I have always believed that education is the key to such things.'

'And books made you think of this?'

'Well. Yes. I'm hardly going to be speaking from experience. I will be referring to scientific texts.'

'You will find no such texts here. Anything that I have on the topic is less…scientific.'

He should not have said that. It was an inappropriate bridge too far. She took a sharp breath.

She looked past him, her eyes trained on the shelves past his shoulder. 'I prefer novels.'

'There are certainly novels that contain such things.'

She turned to him and arched a brow in censure. 'None that I would be interested in.'

'A scientist to your soul?'

'Not *only*. I am interested in all forms of education. But yes. My leaning definitely runs towards the scientific.'

He stood from the chair and went to the shelf, took out a book and held it out towards her. She stared at him for a moment, and then crossed the space, taking it from his hands. Their fingers brushed. And need, stark and hot, rioted through him. Her cheeks went pink, evidence that she felt the same heat that he did.

'This is a book about speculations on the origins of the universe. You might enjoy it.'

'That sounds like it might be sacrilegious.'

'Perhaps it is. I have always been fond of the profane.'

She looked up at him from beneath her lashes. 'Have you?'

'Yes.'

'I will take the book. Thank you. And I... I have your permission? I just wish that I could help the children. And I think that perhaps giving them some scientific basis to understand... That it might help. As I am attempting to bring them through this time alone.'

'Is that a judgement?'

'You know that it is. And yet it isn't. I try... I try to allow space for your loss.'

'And yet?'

'In the meantime the children suffer.'

He was not immune to her words. But he did not think she knew, not truly, of suffering. And the kinds of suffering a child could endure when they were subject to the whims of a parent.

'I see. And what would you have me do?'

'Comfort them.'

'As you did me last night?'

She was goading him, and he did not care for it, pushing his mind to places he did not wish it to go. And so he struck back.

'Your Grace, that was a mistake. I behaved with impropriety.'

'Indeed.'

'I thought to comfort you, as I might one of the children.'

She was icy in her speech when she said that. And he knew that she was a liar. The colour in her cheeks rose high.

'As a child? Is that how you see me?'

'No, Your Grace. But my impulse was to treat you in the same fashion as the children when they have a difficult day.'

'And would you offer me comfort now, Mary?'

'Miss Smith,' she corrected.

'For today has been difficult. Do I not deserve some comfort? The touch of your hand?'

Her breath quickened. 'Your Grace...'

She wanted him. It was apparent. It had been last night when she had knelt before him. The gesture might have been intended to be one of comfort, but it had shifted.

He knew that it would've been easy enough to turn it into a seduction.

But she resisted. And he had to remember that this was a game, not something he intended to follow through with.

Yet she was so close.

And it didn't feel like a game. Not right then. He'd wanted only to be the one in control here, to prove if he pushed things she would falter and not him.

He had forgotten why he was doing this. He had forgotten why he was trying to get her on her back foot.

He had forgotten he was trying to win anything. Because he could smell her. A delicate scent of wildflowers and her sweet skin.

Because she looked so soft he thought he might die from it.

Because he wanted. In a way that transcended everything he'd ever experienced before. Because he wanted in a way that transcended control.

He touched her chin. With his thumb pressed firmly down there, before gripping her tightly by adding his forefinger.

Then he moved his thumb up to the soft pad of

her lower lip, and she gasped. She didn't move away from him.

'Perhaps this is what I want. For you to comfort me as I did you.'

'West,' she whispered.

It was beautiful. To hear her say that.

Because that was when he knew. Knew that he had got through another layer.

He had not touched a living woman in a very long time.

He had last touched Jane after the life had drained out of her. He had knelt by that bed, that blood-soaked bed, and put his forehead against her hand.

And in that moment all he'd had was a wordless apology that was wrenched from his soul as a cry of anguish.

And it hadn't been this.

Of course it hadn't.

He traced the edge of her lip, and then let his thumb rest at the centre, applying pressure.

Her eyelids fluttered downward. 'Yes,' he said. 'Very good.'

He hadn't been conscious of saying that until the words had left his mouth.

He might be testing her control, but she had already gone beyond the bounds of his.

Her tongue darted out, moistened her top lip, and

brushed the edge of his thumb. He groaned, need roaring through him like a lion.

A wild beast that had no business in England, let alone in him.

He took a step towards her, and it was like she came awake.

Just as she had done last night. As if the impropriety of the situation had hit her with the force of a cannon blast.

'I will adjourn to my room,' she said.

He dropped his hand to his side and moved away from her.

'Don't forget your book.'

'I don't... Thank you. Thank you.'

'Mary, you could stay.'

It was a reckless thing to say.

He was never reckless. And yet now he was.

'I can't. I can't, and you want to know that. I... I am your employee, Your Grace. And it has never been in the best interest of a woman to go from governess to whore. I certainly will not be taking that step.'

She turned away from him and fled. And this time she didn't even close the door behind her. She left it open.

He cursed, leaning against the bookshelf, his cock raging.

He wanted her.

He wanted her beyond the telling of it. And he knew full well that he couldn't have her.

He knew. Because he had rules, and wanting a woman was no excuse to violate them. How was he any different from Pelham?

How was he any different from his own father?

Everything in its place, until the minute he wanted something else.

Perhaps he was so bloody good because he had never been tested.

She tested him. And he was failing.

No. The Duke of Westmere did not fail.

He would not fail.

Chapter Eleven

After his correspondence in the morning he took his horse out riding and sought fiercely to erase the interaction he'd had with Miss Mary Smith from his mind.

He had not intended to play that game with her, and yet there was something in the way she had looked down when he stood.

Whether she knew it or not, she was sending him a signal. Letting him know what kind of lover she was.

Perhaps she did know.

It would be laughable, truly, if after her speech about how seducing him would be much simpler than becoming a governess in an attempt to con money from him, she was in fact attempting to seduce him.

It would not be *impossible* for her to have come armed with the knowledge of his tastes.

While he had not practised them during his marriage—he had been a faithful husband, for all the good it had done him—his reputation in the clubs of London stretched back years.

In his twenties, he had rather exhausted the supply of harlots interested in his favoured forms of power exchange.

And married women.

It would not be impossible to find out exactly how to appeal to him.

And yet he doubted it. There was something untried in the way she had reacted. Not innocent, but not calculated either.

But this was yet another thing he kept ruthlessly contained in its channel.

He could remember, very clearly, his uncle speaking to him sternly after the death of his father.

'You are the Duke. Undeniably. You outrank me in every way. But having watched your father tear apart my sister's life, having watched him wreak havoc on all of his children, I will speak to you on the subject. The only kindness he ever did my sister was keeping his unusual tastes confined to mistresses and brothels. There are things that you do with a harlot that you must never ask of a lady wife.'

And he, all of sixteen and horrified by the mention of a brothel, and by the fantasies that rolled through his mind at night when sleep did not claim him, had only stood there, looking stone-faced at the back wall.

But he had taken it to heart.

And when he had seen to his instruction regarding his baser appetites, he had asked one of the harlots which acts were not permitted with wives.

She had laughed.

'This is why I'd never seek to be a proper lady. I should be grateful, I suppose, that I was born far beneath such considerations. I would rather suck a cock than spend my days hosting tea parties.'

And that, he had learned, was one of the things that wives did not do.

He had known what he was giving up to be married. But he had seen it as an easy enough task.

He'd given up one in favour of gaining another.

And it was a chance to prove his superior control. He was better than his father, and he would always have that assurance.

He never raised his voice to his children, nor his hand. And never to his wife, regardless of how things had soured.

He was never unfaithful. And he'd never asked for her to…

He wondered, not for the first time, if he had done the wrong thing somehow.

And yet he could not take that on board. He dismissed it. Harshly and brutally.

He urged his horse forward, tapping his flanks, and then stopped him short when he looked down over the rolling hills and saw three figures picking through the grass. His two children, and a woman with very bright red hair.

She was wearing a different dress to the one she'd

had on yesterday, this one a pale colour that lit her up as a beacon across the way.

He should turn away and leave them. His children's lessons were not his concern. It was why he had need of a governess.

And the governess was why he had need of a punishing ride.

And yet he found himself riding his horse towards them.

He had never come across his children on their outings. The previous governesses had always kept their charges confined to the garden.

And this was far and away from the more civilised places on the estate. There were foxes, badgers and even wolves out there.

And he allowed himself to feel angry that Mary had brought them out this far without speaking to him first. Yes, she had said that she was taking them out, but why would he ever assume that she would go beyond the confines of the walls?

He picked up the pace, the intensity of the horse's gait increasing.

He saw when they heard him. They stopped, looking in his direction with wide eyes.

He stopped the horse and got off.

'Steady,' he said to the beast, putting his hand on the stallion's neck. The horse obeyed.

He strode towards them, his dark greatcoat blowing in the wind. 'And what is it you are doing out this way?'

'Your Grace,' she said, nodding.

'Father,' said Elizabeth, giving him a curtsy.

And Michael said nothing, looking away from him.

Did his son hate him?

He'd hated his own father. Perhaps a man was doomed to be hated by his son.

'We are about our botany lesson,' Mary said, wrinkling her nose, which had grown pink from the sun and was far more interesting to him than he should like.

'As I mentioned last night, I have a great affinity for all subjects.'

'You did,' he agreed. 'And yet I did not know that you meant to take the children out into the wilderness.'

She did something that he could not recall anyone ever doing before. She laughed at him. 'The wilderness? We can quite see Attingham itself from here. We are not in the wilderness.'

'And yet did you not consider the dangers? There are wolves here.'

'I don't think there are. I believe wolves have been extinct in England since the seventeen-hundreds.'

She was arguing with him in the broad light of day in front of his children, this woman who worked for him, and he ought to put a stop to it, but, as ever, he found he was far too...interested.

In where it might go. In what she might say next.

He knew that to be true, and yet he also knew there was danger everywhere. 'Wolves come in many forms, Miss Smith, as I think you know.'

Whether he was warning her about himself or some other danger, he did not know.

'We've been looking at flowers,' said Michael. His tone was staunch. 'Mary has taught us a great many things.'

'*Mary?*' He looked at her. 'Has she given you permission to use her Christian name?'

She had scolded him for it just last night.

'Yes,' said Elizabeth.

For her part, *Mary*, as he would now think of her evermore, looked at him with a small amount of shame. 'I am attempting to ease some boundaries between us.'

'I see. I am rather fond of boundaries. They keep everything in their rightful place. And that is quite an important thing, do you not think so, Mary?'

Her name on his tongue should have been the most common thing. For her name was dreadfully overused as to be one of the most common names. And yet it was like springtime, but shot through with something more.

Something forbidden. Something bright and new.

And *nothing* was forbidden to him. He could call one of his employees by her Christian name if he chose.

Still.

It felt tinged with impropriety. Perhaps because the only times he had ever called a woman by her first name, and her his, was when they were lovers. And even then, only his wife had ever called him *Samuel*.

Even then, it had been infrequent.

'I do not believe that you and I have had the same conversation, Your Grace.' Twin spots of colour rose high in her cheeks.

'I do not believe it is necessary.'

All remained unspoken, but he could see that she had perceived his message all the same. If his children were allowed informal address, he certainly was. He was a duke. Not to be disallowed anything. Not anything.

'Your Grace,' she said, 'I can assure you that the children are very safe.'

'I do not feel that is your determination to make.'

'Your Grace,' she said, 'I beg, if you are concerned for our safety, accompany us as we journey into the wood.'

'Do you think I'm not about other business?'

She looked up at him, her eyes—they were green, he noticed just then, the same colour as the trees around them—glimmering. 'I'm certain you are. But what business could be more pressing than our safety?'

'Nothing, of course,' he said.

He tethered his horse to the nearest tree. She was challenging him, and he well knew it. He did not know why he was rising to the challenge. Only she spoke to him in a manner no one else dared. In a manner no one else ever had.

And perhaps the problem was that above all else there was a relentless, aching dullness to his life. There was grief. There was sadness. There was the feeling that his children were like strangers to him.

But it was like staring into the grey mist that covered the countryside and seeing nothing more. Nothing more than mist, nothing more than resolute, opaque sameness. And she was a bright speck in all that grey. Not in the sense that many might mean that. He was not sentimental. He did not mean that she was some sort of beacon in the darkness, only that she was different. And these past months had been the only time in his life he'd felt lost in something he could not shift or change or fix since he was a child.

He hated the lack of control more than he hated anything. Everything was spinning out of his grasp.

At least this was new. At least this was a problem of sorts. Something to latch onto. Something to focus on.

A fight, in many ways. And it fired his blood.

And it also sounded a warning inside of him, for he well knew what she was.

His employee. His children's governess.

His children seemed content in a way they had not with any of the previous women in her position.

They needed stability. Above all else.

And he was not a man who could afford to compromise himself or what he had found.

'I am no expert in botany,' he said. 'But I am expert on these grounds. Perhaps, however, you will find something to teach me.'

She pinned her arms behind her back, a pose that brought illicit images to the fore of his mind. Her hands pinned tightly, her breasts offered up to him…

'A possibility, Your Grace, and one we cannot discount.'

He realised that his children were looking at him as if he were an unrecognisable beast set down into their midst.

And he thought he ought to turn his focus to them rather than thinking untoward thoughts about their governess.

'Is there something you wish to ask me, children?' he said, addressing them both.

'You never walk with us,' said Elizabeth.

'And that is not a question,' he responded.

But something like guilt lanced his chest, and he could not explain it. He should feel no guilt for how he conducted himself with his children. He had never harmed them. Not once. And he never would.

They did not live in fear of him. He was a father who was truly only ever a father in their presence. They did not witness the messy broken pieces of any love affairs, they did not have to bear the brunt of his anger or frustration.

They had never once seen his grief.

He was a stable, steady figure in their lives, and he would feel no regret for that.

'These are all edible plants,' said Mary, gesturing towards lichen and a collection of berries, a particular sort of green. 'If ever you were to find yourself lost, you could eat these.' She straightened. 'Not these.' She pointed to some white berries on the end of the bush. 'And it is wise to never take risks with mushrooms and other fungi. Many are edible, but it is important that you not make a mistake.'

'And where did you learn these things?' he asked, unable to help himself. He was intrigued by her, damn it all.

'The Highlands,' she said. 'We often hunted for food there. I did. For my family.'

He looked at her with speculation. 'This is something you speak freely about?'

'You are already aware of my origins. I see no reason not to speak freely of it to the children.'

'Mary is very interesting,' said Elizabeth. 'She has stories. And not just made-up stories like the others. Not just fairy tales. She had *adventures*.'

Her cheeks went pink, and she did not look at him. 'Childhood in the Scottish Highlands is different than childhood in England. At least, for English nobility.

My own adventures would likely seem a bit shocking to you.'

Then she looked at him. And the small smile on her lips undid him.

She was filled with humour, and he could not recall the last time someone had looked at him as if they might laugh at him. Perhaps never.

'You think my own childhood was not filled with adventures?' It had been filled with terror, it was true. But he and his brother had made great fun of nothing when they could escape the estate. They had wandered these very grounds, these woods.

All of the things she knew, he knew better. About this place.

'My brother and I used to pretend to be highwaymen. I think the maids did not thank us for our skulduggery.'

'You and Uncle Luke?' Elizabeth asked, and he became aware that of course his children were listening, and that also they did not know these stories. But he had not thought they would find them interesting. Or rather, it made him feel strange to admit to himself that he had never considered what they might think of stories of him as a child.

'Yes,' he said. 'Uncle Luke.'

He saw his brother only rarely. He preferred London and did not care for the memories associated with their country home. He could not blame him. His brother's wife was a lovely woman, and their children well-mannered.

Their life seemed smooth and happy in a way that West's own had never been.

He did not resent his brother that. His brother was the spare, not the heir, and therefore was not beset by the same responsibilities.

But he had been equally punished by their father's temper. Luke deserved some ease.

'Your Uncle Luke had a stick that he quite favoured, that he thought resembled a pistol. His very favourite thing was to run around the grounds terrorising all and sundry with it. He liked to jump down out of trees and ambush me. But I had a wooden sword.'

He did not often think about the brighter things in his past. It was easy to think of his father's fists, not the time he'd spent with his brother terrorising the staff.

But perhaps it was the bright spot before him that had brought it to mind.

The woman in question gazed up at him, her lips curving slightly.

'Well, this is a moment of true education. Even formidable dukes were once small boys.'

Michael looked dazed by this information. And suddenly, looking down at his son, he imagined himself at that age. And his father, a couple of inches shorter than West was now, but nonetheless formidable, bringing his fist down on him, and his reaction was such a violent rejection of the image that he could scarcely breathe.

How was it possible to unleash your anger on something so small and innocent? He had never thought of himself as such.

But now, as a man, the fragility of an eight-year-old boy seemed impossibly cruel.

'Yes,' he said. 'Even dukes start as children.'

He forged ahead and realised he did not know what Mary intended. But then, she could not possibly know, as she had never been here before.

'There's a clearing up ahead. And a pond. Perhaps you might enjoy seeing that?'

'Yes,' the children said in staggered chorus.

They seemed happy. And it had never once occurred to him that being in his presence might make them happy. They always seemed a bit aggrieved when in his presence otherwise. They had loved Jane, and who could blame them? He had loved her too.

She was silly and whimsical, a delicate bird of a woman who had fluttered from room to room and had seemed insubstantial in many ways—many ways that now felt confirmed. It had always felt as if she might slip away at any moment, and indeed she had.

But she had been bright, and the children had loved her dearly. She had been his companion for many years. And the loss of that was something he felt keenly.

But they seemed happy to have him with them now, and that felt like another new thing.

Another bit of brightness to pierce the grey.

They forged through the woods, until the sun pierced through from the other side of the dense copse. 'There it is. Just up ahead.'

Both children raced forward, and there was something about watching their childlike freedom, the way they moved their arms like windmills and ran all spread out, not keeping to a straight line, that did something strange to his chest.

And that left him standing with Mary. She looked at him, a strange sort of glimmer in her eyes. 'It was good of you to join us.'

'You left me with no choice.'

'You are a duke. You always have a choice.'

It was said lightly, but something smarted beneath it. He could not pinpoint it.

'I am ready to fend off wolves if need be.'

'That would be a sight.'

He looked to her. 'Do you doubt my ability?'

And this time she didn't bother to suppress her smile. 'Naturally not. You have a wooden sword.'

'I have a great deal more than that.'

He had never in all of his life bantered with a woman. And he found it easy to do with her. Strangely, the last time he could remember having a free conversation with someone was with his brother, whom he had only just been thinking of.

He was not, and never had been, the toast of the *tonne*. In the sense that he was a duke, yes. He had been a target for marriage-minded mothers, and it had been about his title and not his personality, he was well aware. He offered security, he offered wealth. Status. And that was enough. He did not need to be amusing. He had an intensity about him as a lover, and that was the thing women liked about him the most. But it was nothing he and his wife had ever connected on. He had done his duty by her. He had protected her. Mary seemed to find him amusing. However, he was not certain she was laughing with him.

'Yes, you should ask the wolves to address you as *Your Grace*, and genuflect accordingly.'

'You should look quite pretty if you genuflected.'

He was a man of supreme control. And he had not meant to say that. The idea of this woman on her knees in supplication before him was intoxicating in ways he could not afford to ponder.

The image of her, down before him in the study, assaulted him again and it was far too easy for him to make her nude. Smooth and perfect and utterly his.

Her face went scarlet, colour bleeding down her neck, disappearing behind the modest neckline of her dress.

She was not unaware of the other meaning beneath that comment.

It was clear by her response. Nor was she unaffected by it.

'A compliment,' he said. 'Nothing more.'

'A shame then,' she said, not meeting his eyes, 'that you will never see me looking pretty.'

'I didn't say you were not equally lovely when not kneeling in supplication.'

He should not push this either. And yet he found he wanted to. Because this strange moment, outdoors in the middle of the day, with his horse tethered half a league away, and his children laughing and frolicking around a pond he had not been to since childhood, when he and his brother were trying to play, and forget. Forget who their father was, and that he was waiting back home with strong drink on his breath and violence in his fists.

And he was here, with this woman. Mary Smith. Who was lying about her name and, he was certain, concealing things about her background.

But she was beautiful, and she treated him as no one had for years.

She did look up at him then, met his gaze with something like fury, even while her voice remained measured. 'What a relief to know you find me pretty. I don't know how I should have persevered otherwise.'

He felt his own mouth curving upward. A foreign sensation. A foreign feeling. In amusement.

Amusement, and a sort of dark attraction.

'Was there a man back in Scotland?'

Her face went ashen. As if a light had been snuffed out, and he hated that.

'I was thirteen when I left,' she said.

A girl. Close enough to Elizabeth's age.

'And you have managed to gain that much education in so few years?'

'Yes. As I have been teaching the children, when something feels like a gift, when you never felt owed it, or guaranteed, it feels like a treasure. And you do not squander such treasure.'

'You learned everything you could?'

'Everything. I did at least twice the amount of schoolwork every year, and I did not leave on school holidays. I was fortunate. A rare thing, for a girl to be able to be educated in such a fashion, and there are few places that provide such. My family never could have—never would have—but the leader of my clan saw potential in me and honoured my dreams.'

'And you knew then that you wished to forgo a traditional life? No husband or family?'

He knew everyone in society. And he was tired of them. It was all games and doublespeak. All completely disingenuous. They all knew each other and knew of each other. Everyone knew his father had been a monster, but his father had been a duke. So nothing had been done.

It had been known to many that Jane was occupied elsewhere. But not to him. He commanded respect, unless there was some greater social amusement at work.

He was tired of everyone in his acquaintance.

But he did not know Mary.

And he felt compelled to know her more. It was the first time in so many years he had felt that way about anyone.

'A life as a wife is a life spent in a cage. And while in your part of society that cage is often an especially lovely one, in the world I'm from, it is not. There was no future for me there.'

'Some might argue that life itself is a cage regardless. We must all play a role, after all.'

'Some might argue that, I suppose. But a duke is in perhaps a rather interesting position to attempt to argue from. You are the keeper of these things. Much more so than most.'

'I am the keeper of an ancient title that must be carried on. There is duty and propriety that I must observe, whether you believe that to be true, or a burden, or not.'

'But you have choice, and the way that the world would respond to you would be entirely different than a woman who made the same choices. You are correct, there is an element of a cage whatever I do. Whatever a woman does. But I have the freedom of my time when I am in my room alone. And I would not barter that.'

'And will you tell my daughter these things?'

'Your daughter will likely be happier if she makes a good match. Most girls dream of finding a husband. I lived a life that made that dream quite impossible. But you… Surely you know the reputation of any man and his family who might seek her hand in the years to come. Surely you will be able to protect her.'

Everything in him went grim. Because he could hear what she was saying. Really hear it.

A marriage to a man like his own father was a life sentence to misery. His mother had lived that misery. He would never, ever consign his daughter to such a fate, and if he were to discover that her husband raised his fists to her, he would kill him.

But he could see then the concerns that she spoke of, clearly.

He did not worry about such a thing for Michael. Michael who would be the Duke.

But Elizabeth would have to make a good match, and that meant so much more than society defined it as.

'I take your meaning,' he said.

'I'm glad you do.'

She was a woman who had seen cruelty. He could see that clearly.

'It is time, likely, for the children to get back to their lessons.'

'We have a picnic lunch waiting for us back in the garden.'

'Good. I will escort you back there.

'You will come and meet me in my study this afternoon. And we will speak about your plans to walk about the grounds, and the safety concerns.'

'Yes, Your Grace.'

Mary went and beckoned the children back to them and they began to head back on the path that would take them home to Attingham.

'Father, it has been a lovely day,' said Elizabeth, her face alight with joy he hadn't seen in far too long.

He could see Mary flush, but this time it was with pleasure. She cared a great deal that the children had a good time. He could see that.

He did not care whether or not the children had a good time. It was not about that. Safety, and whether or not they were about their studies, that was what mattered. Everything in its proper place. And he was not certain his children's proper place was beyond the walls of the garden.

And yet he would not make them come in now.

'Three o'clock sharp,' he said.

'Yes, Your Grace.'

And there was something in that acquiescence that he found sweet.

He turned and rode away from her, and made his way back to the estate. His grooms took the horse, and led him back to the stables.

His heart was thundering.

She was insolent, was Mary Smith. And he was even more certain than ever that Smith was not her last name. He imagined it was one reason she actually had the children call her by her first name. He wondered if she had difficulty answering to it regularly.

If she sometimes did not recall the ruse, or her ears did not turn naturally towards Smith.

He did not like insolent women. When he played games with them in the brothels, he preferred for them to be perfectly obedient. And yet there was something about the way that Mary defied him that excited him.

Fired his blood.

Jane would've seen that as a perversion. Or perhaps she wouldn't have.

He did not know his wife. It was something that would haunt him until he died. He had not truly known her at all.

When he made his way back into the house, the cry of the babe was rending the air in two.

'Mrs Brown,' he shouted, forgetting himself. Forgetting to ring the bell.

'Why have we not found a new wet nurse?'

'Oh, Your Grace,' Mrs Brown said, moving quickly through the room. 'We have been searching...'

'Have we no safety measures in place for if that occurs?'

'The governess and I are meant to attend the babe if the wet nurse is not at hand, but I was seeing to—'

'You have responsibilities, Mrs Brown, I know.'

And Mary was out on the property. Of course.

'This will not do.'

'Your Grace...'

'I do not wish to hear the child. Nor do I wish to be responsible for the care of the child, do you understand?'

'Yes, Your Grace,' said Mrs Brown.

And he knew she did not understand. She never would.

And he was caught between giving an explanation and knowing that he never could offer one.

It was untenable. Utterly untenable.

And perhaps his anger wasn't warranted when it came to Mary, but she had left the house and she had not made arrangements with Mrs Brown, clearly. And how dare she lecture him on the babe and his needs when she had forgotten him?

God help Mary Smith when she appeared before him today at three sharp. Because there were things that needed to be settled. And he would see that they were.

Chapter Twelve

Something in her felt wild and reckless as she made her way to the Duke's study.

The back of her throat felt hollow, a strange metallic taste on her tongue.

Her heart was thundering rapidly, even though she had not run. She stood, her wrist poised, her fist ready to knock on the door.

'If you are standing outside, do come in.'

A smile touched her lips. He had known that she would be on time. And he was obviously completely mindful of the minute.

She opened the door. 'Your Grace.'

'How is it, Mary, that you have seen fit to lecture me on the care of the babe, in this very spot, when you yourself did not see to his care this afternoon?'

'Your Grace?'

'The babe was crying. No one was here to tend to the infant. Mrs Brown had other responsibilities to

see to and had not made it to see the child, and when
I arrived at the house he was inconsolable.'

Her temper ignited, and swiftly. The child was not
solely her responsibility and if he could hear him Mrs
Brown could have too. But, above all else, he had
been there.

'Surely it would not hurt your lofty station to hold
your own child?'

And she realised the moment she had said that that
her words had run away with her. No matter what she
thought, he was...the Duke. And she could not speak
to him in that fashion.

'I'm sorry,' she said swiftly.

He was a man in grief. A man who had lost his wife,
and she could see that the babe occupied a complicated space in everyone's life. But she could not help
but pity the small child who had done nothing but be
born. The child who had no stake in what had become
of the woman who had birthed him. And yet was re-
viled by everyone around him.

'And yet you are not,' he said. 'You think that you
can challenge me. You did so when you were out in
the fields with my children. You question my authority in front of them.'

'I confess that I have not had so much interaction
with the master of the house over the course of my
tenure as governess for other families.'

'I assume that their mother was not dead.'

'You assume correctly. And I apologise. I have never taken employment with a duke and...'

'You do not respect me. Nor my title.'

'I understand the position that you occupy.'

'You do not observe it.'

'Have I not spoken to you using appropriate honorifics?'

'Certainly you have, and yet your tone remains insolent.'

'You called me Mary.' She let out a sharp breath. 'If we are to speak of respect then let us speak of it being mutual. I might not be a duke, but I am something.'

He said nothing. He only regarded her closely. Intently.

Her heart was fluttering, and she was angry. So angry. And yet there was something else. A strange sort of fierce excitement that kicked up within her as she challenged him.

'Your children respect you, Your Grace, and yet I do not get the impression that they know you.'

'Children are not meant to know their parents. They are meant only to respect them. I, as a father, am required only to provide them with that which they need. The tools to succeed in life. And I am meant to present a figure that they can respect. I could not do that with my own father, and I will be damned if I fail my children on that score.'

She could see that he regretted saying that. That he

did not feel he owed her an explanation for anything and was upset with himself that he had done so.

'My own father was a cruel man,' she said. 'And my mother was ground to dust beneath his cruelty. The only people that she had dominion over were her children, and she was not kind to us. Perhaps it was born of fear. I cannot hold her in equal responsibility as I do my father. And yet I will confess to you that I have never seen kind parenting, apart from the families that I have worked for. Even then, it is a distant sort of love. It is better, I admit, than the sort of actions my parents took in my life.'

'You say this as if we might be of one accord. As if we might understand one another.'

'You had a cruel father. As did I. What is there to misunderstand between us?'

'I am a duke. And you, Mary, are a charlatan.'

The way he said her name sent a strange shiver through her body. It did every time and it was why she hated it. Not because she felt disrespected, but because it made her feel…warm.

'My name is Mary McLaren, if you must know. I have not left her behind out of fear, but because I cannot bear to carry the weight of her anymore. I do not wish to think of that life, and I do not wish to be connected to it. Changing my surname cuts that tie between myself and my family.'

'And yet when you are a member of the peerage to

do so would be foolish. Your bloodline, the family line, is essential. Important.'

'The only thing my family ever had to leave me was dirt and poverty and shame. Violence. I've no need of it. And so I've left them.' She was breathing hard. 'I know that you are not a violent man.'

Something glinted in his eyes. It was dangerous, but not dangerous in a way that made her afraid.

'You think you know that about me?'

'Yes. A woman alone in the world must become expert at reading men. I know when a man takes pleasure in hurting others.'

His lips curved. 'An interesting choice of words.'

'You do not wish to break another person's spirit, Your Grace, and that is something I assessed the moment we met. When you correctly interpreted my accent, I became deeply invested in what you might seek to do with such information. If you might wish to simply dismiss me, something that is understandable, or if you might wish to make me pay. To make me suffer. And I did not see that in you. You and I share the common bond that we do not wish to be the cruellest parts of our parents.'

'You speak with me in an extremely familiar fashion.'

'Would you rather I was dishonest? Would you rather I pretended to feel an awe that I simply don't?'

But then he moved towards her, and she felt her words echoing inside of her as a lie.

She was in awe of him.

His beauty, his strength.

She had never in all of her life appreciated masculine beauty, and when he strode towards her in the field only an hour ago, with his coat billowing behind him, she had known something new.

Something twisted inside of her.

And that urge she had felt to test his strength had become stronger.

All these years she had feared male strength.

And yet. She was not naïve about intercourse. It had been forced on her, after all.

She knew what it felt like to have the weight of a man on top of her. To have him thrusting inside of her.

It had been painful, and it had been pure humiliation. Fear. Nothing about it had borne a resemblance to either a clinical act of procreation, which should be divorced of feeling and emotion, or the soft romantic dreams of the girls at boarding school.

They had talked about handsome men, words of poetry. Of being kissed and walking in gardens. They had dreamed of the sort of touch she hadn't truly believed in.

And all the while she had kept her secrets close to her breast. For no one could know that she was not a maid. No one could know that her virginity was long since lost in a muddy field.

She did not wonder about those things, but she did wonder about his strength. What it would feel like to have it surround her. But not used against her. She did wonder that.

And she did not know if she was filled with a strange sort of hopeful joy at the realisation that she could experience still this strange, mystical wonder at the mysteries between men and women, or horror that the years had faded away something that she had considered to be one of her greatest protections.

She was not naïve. And she was not foolish. She would never put herself in that sort of position again.

And yet she found herself looking at his eyes, his mouth, the strong column of his throat.

Found herself compelled by his hands, large and strong-looking.

The way that he had ridden up on the horse, demanding much of the beast. The way he'd held his riding crop in his hands...

'Give me the truth then. What is it you think of men like me?'

'I have never known a man like you.'

It was the truth. Nothing more, nothing less, and yet she was appalled to have had it exit her mouth.

'Have you not?'

'As I said,' she said, trying to recover herself, 'I have never worked for a duke.'

'And what sort of men do you know, Mary?'

'Small men,' she said. 'Men who hurt women. And men who enjoy the subjugation of those around them. The humiliation.'

'They are not men. My father was such a man. And his primary sin was never knowing where to channel the various vices he possessed. A man in possession of much power must know how to wield it. Anger can be expended, but never upon your wife and children. Never upon those weaker than yourself. Power can be wielded, but never for the sake of diminishing another. It is men who never grow beyond boys who do not understand this.'

She could see that he had put a great deal of thought into this.

'Then trust me to take your children into the woods, to have fun with them—trust *me*. Is that not allowing something to be in its rightful place? They had fun today out in the wood.'

'Botany is not a necessary pursuit.'

'No. But it was fun. I… Your Grace, I am very, very sorry for the loss of your wife. The children lost something of their childhood when they lost their mother. And I know all too well what it is to lose your innocence. Your youth. Before its time.'

She felt breathless standing before him.

Talking to him down by the pond had been the strangest experience. For he'd felt nearly…tame for a moment. And then she'd seen the beast. That dangerous thing in him, and it did not make her want to turn away.

There had been a note of steel in his voice when he had spoken of her supplication, and yet it was different. Different to men who wished to harm women.

There was something velvet and enticing about it. An invitation to test his strength. In a way that appealed.

For the first time, she imagined what it might be like for a man to touch her. Her face, her mouth.

It was far too easy to imagine those large hands drifting along her jawline, the edge of her lip.

She looked up at him, a gasp making her breath hitch.

'I thank you,' he said. 'For the connection you have forged with the children. Even in such a short time. But you must avail yourself to the child.'

'The babe. The babe who does not have a name.'

'You will not speak to me of such things.'

His voice held a bite that resonated inside of her.

His commands were infuriating, but at the same time they made something foreign echo within her.

She did not understand the magic he possessed. The thing in him that called to something in her that was long dead.

Whispering to her that he could resurrect something she had never been allowed to fully understand.

And it was a temptation.

Yet she suddenly felt undone by it.

She had never considered herself a blushing maiden. She was not one, after all. She had felt wizened and world-weary by comparison to her contemporaries, and yet he made her feel innocent again. He made her want something she had no name for.

It was not the simple, sweet yearning of a blushing innocent, that much she knew. And she could not fully form an image in her head of what she desired of this man.

It was frightening and compelling all at once. It was like the first blush of something that she had never been allowed to truly have. And she wasn't sure what she should do about it. If she should move closer to him or flee.

You definitely should not move closer. There is no justification for that. If you want stability. If you want to stay here, to stay with the children...

The children.

Perhaps she should not have shared with them about Scotland. But they were so entranced by it. It gave them something new to think about. Something beyond simply lessons.

And she could feel their sadness like a cloak around them, and she wanted so badly to do something to ease that sadness. Their mother had died. And there would be no easy way to fix that sort of sorrow.

But she wanted to introduce happiness into their lives again. And she had remembered better things about Scotland than she had for years. Her mind had already been brought back to the lowest points multiple times since she had come to this place. But something about that had allowed her to remember the good.

The beauty of the mountains. The way it had felt to run free with her brothers over the fields. To look for food in the forest. To sit and eat in the waning sunlight, away from their parents.

Every moment had not been dark.

It was the magic of childhood.

The way that you focused on the sun and the freedom, and the wilderness around you, even when there were many great and terrible things.

She wanted to give them the sunlight.

There was something horrid in having your innocence ripped from you.

And what had become of her was only one way that could happen. Death, grief, anything that destroyed the magic of the world could bring you to that place. There was something about trying to give it to them that brought out the sun in her own mind. Her own memory.

It was magical in a way nothing had been for a very long time.

She couldn't leave.

She looked at him, his stern expression, the strong line of his jaw. She begged him in her heart to stay away from her.

Because he must understand. He must know. And he seemed like a man who obeyed the rules...except he had called her pretty.

Their eyes met then, and she wondered.

If they were both lost.

The idea terrified her.

And thrilled her in a way that nothing had ever before in her memory.

Chapter Thirteen

Their every meeting for the rest of the week felt tense, as if a thread stretched between them that was likely to snap.

West was no stranger to attraction. He understood what it was to desire someone sexually.

He desired *her*.

But there was something else that mingled with his desire for her. The taste of the forbidden, perhaps, because he was a man who always kept himself in control.

He did not dally with staff. He had not visited his more raw sexual urges upon his wife.

And he did not engage harlots in conversation.

There was something dangerous about this.

It was why he found himself wandering the halls now. He couldn't sleep. Visions of her assaulted him.

Many men would think it prudent and acceptable to satisfy their desires with a member of staff, though the governess was frowned upon. If only because she had such a close association to children.

It was acceptable for a man of his status to have affairs. But usurping the position of your wife was not so easily accepted.

He had opted for fidelity because he had decided it was best to keep himself in line.

But the fact was, Jane was gone. He did not envision himself living the life of a celibate.

He needed to make his way to London soon, needed to find a harlot who enjoyed sucking cock and being used hard.

If he was going to return to that way of things, then he would have his needs met.

But when he thought of a woman on her knees before him, opening her delicate lips, it was only Mary that he could see. She dressed demurely. She did not dress to attract male attention, that was certain, and yet it was as if his need took it as a challenge.

To try and gather visions of the shape of her. The way that her creamy skin would look uncovered.

The infant began to wail.

It felt like a puncture wound. For once his mind had been turned towards pleasant things, and the infant was intruding.

He waited. Waited and listened, for the rest of the household to rouse, but he could hear no one.

He needed to get a different wet nurse. This was a

far too common occurrence. It was her job, before it was Mary's. And he should never have to…

He couldn't stand it.

With gritted teeth he strode through the hall, making his way to the infant's room.

And, right as he did, a vision in white appeared in the darkened corridor.

Her red hair was down, and with the light of the candle she was holding he could see that her eyes were round.

'Your Grace,' she said. 'I am terribly sorry. I…'

'I… It is not ideal, but it is not your fault.'

'I… I should have been faster.'

'It is fine.' He walked into the bedroom, and she came in behind him. He was well aware that by the standards of society this was shocking.

But he was jaded enough that he simply didn't care.

Or perhaps he wished to court impropriety.

Not that he could think properly of impropriety with the child screaming like this.

He stood at the edge of the room.

She looked at him. 'Do you not wish to gather your child? I can get the milk if you would like…'

'No. I do not wish to hold him.'

She frowned. She went to the crib and picked him up, her movements awkward.

'I do not have much experience with babies. I have only ever cared for children.'

'Of course,' he said. It made sense.

He had experience with babies. Going back as far as Elizabeth, of course.

He could likely offer her some assistance.

'I will get milk.'

'Do you know how?'

He frowned. He could wake the staff. And anyway, how difficult could it be? Did he know how? He was a man who managed vast estates.

'Why don't I accompany you to the kitchen?' she said. 'I will bring the child.'

His muscles tensed. 'There's no need…'

'Come,' she said.

And he found himself following her down the hall, transfixed by the sight of her in her dressing gown. It gave him a better idea of her shape, and when she passed by a moonlit window he could see the silhouette of her waist, her lovely pear-shaped arse and slender legs.

She was holding the babe.

And he was touching depravity.

Something he had always avoided. Something he had always believed necessary to stay away from, and yet he felt his defences were diminished.

Had it been that long since he had a woman, or was it simply her?

He was so rarely in the kitchen, it almost felt like visiting another home.

And he was galled by how useless he felt. How she had read him, far too accurately.

He did not know how to prepare milk for an infant.

'If you could hold him just for a moment,' she said.

'No.'

'He's your son, Your Grace.'

And there, in the darkness of the kitchen, he said the one thing he'd never said before. Not out loud.

'He's not my son.'

'What?'

She looked shocked. The child was fractious in her arms, and he gritted his teeth. 'He is not my son. I am not so cold-hearted that I would deny my own flesh and blood a name or affection because his mother died in childbirth.'

She looked as if she was trying to do a complicated mathematical equation in her head.

'But cold enough to deny the blood of another man,' she said, slowly.

'Yes.'

It was not so simple. These were the consequences of Jane's actions and, dammit all, he would have rather the child had died.

The thought sliced him open.

But then… Then Jane could have been contrite. She could have decided to be different, or he could have decided to structure their lives differently. He could have returned to the brothels if she'd wanted to have other men.

Or maybe they could have spoken frankly about their desires.

But she had died.

And they had never spoken about it. Not about any of it.

It had been nothing but her, lovelorn and mooning over a man who did not wish to cause scandal by claiming her, by leaving his wife, by stealing the wife of the Duke. A man who would not claim his child.

And it had been West marinating in the humiliation of it, even though no one else would ever know the child wasn't his.

He did. Because he knew exactly when he had last been in his wife's bed. And there was no chance she had conceived the boy with him.

Once she had given him an heir, once Michael had been born, their encounters had grown fewer and fewer.

He had wanted a spare, but she had not attacked the task with any sort of vigour. Conception was not the easiest thing for his wife. She'd had many losses between Elizabeth and Michael.

It was the one thing that made him certain that whatever affair she'd been carrying on with another man had been going on for some time in order to conceive and have a pregnancy that she actually carried to term.

'You are certain…'

'I had not lain with my wife for a year. The child is not mine. And my wife is dead. And what am I to do? She died in childbirth. Everyone knows this. To expose the fact that the infant is not mine is to expose her to censure after her death. The mother of my children. What am I to do? If she were a man, we could simply put her bastard in a school somewhere, and deal with it that way. But she was not a man. She was a woman. And the shame would be endless. For all of us. Her parents are good people, they are good grandparents to my children, and she was a good mother. I have no wish to destroy their memory of her. Nor can I find it in me to care for the evidence of her betrayal, and the child that caused her death.'

'The child didn't…'

'I know that,' he said. 'But how am I to feel?'

'I'm sorry,' she said. 'I didn't know. Your Grace…'

'Mary,' he said. 'Perhaps you should call me West. You are the only living person who knows the truth about this child. And I need your silence.'

'I won't tell anyone. I promise. I promise you I won't.'

'Thank you.'

'West,' she said. 'That is not your Christian name.'

'No. But it is what everyone calls me. My friends. If I had any.'

He tried to say it with humour, but it was true enough.

'I... I didn't know. And I am sorry that I stood in judgement of you.'

With the infant in her arms she checked the stove, which seemed to have a low flame in it already.

She took out a pot, and a jar of milk. She poured a measure of milk into the pot, her movements looking more at ease than he would've imagined, given that she had said she'd never cared for a babe before.

'I would have allowed her to care for her bastard, and I would have laid claim to him. If she had lived. It would've been simple enough. Though I know she wanted to leave me.'

'And the children?'

He felt his soul turn to stone. 'I don't know.'

'Surely she could not have taken your children from you. Your heir.'

'By law, no. But she could have run with them. She might have, if her lover had not cast her aside. We did not have a way to communicate. We did not... She would not have had a child with another man if all had been well. I do not know what was in her mind.'

He could not say what hurt him more. The thought that his wife would have taken the children from him, or that she would have left them. He had watched his children deal with their mother's death. The devastation his children would have felt, knowing their mother might leave them... It destroyed him. The idea that they might have been taken away from him hurt no less. However, he could not say for certain if they might have been happier with their mother.

She, for her flaws, had been warm and lovely.

She had taken tea in the garden with them. She had pieces of her heart that were not frozen, and...

Many of the failures in their life, their marriage, had been his. He had been faithful. But his heart had never been hers.

He often wondered if he had driven her into the arms of another. If he could have stopped it had he been a different man, a different husband.

And yet there was no real healing to be had in thinking of these things.

She had not left.

She had stayed. She had given birth. The child hadn't died.

She had.

And so the babe was here, a burden for him to bear should he want to preserve his wife's reputation. And his own. A man who was made a cuckold, a man who had a cuckoo in his nest was hardly a man who could be looked up to.

Keeping the child, preserving the idea that the child

was his was the best way forward in every way except this. Except…

With the milk finished, Mary turned to him as she fed the infant using a ceramic pot.

'I will see a new wet nurse is found by tomorrow,' he said.

'A good idea. The poor child. I don't think he understands why he has lost his superior food.'

'Perhaps if the wet nurse were not more interested in the man she was seeing he would still have it. A concern for whoever I find to take her place.'

'Not all women are distracted by men,' she said.

'Is that so?'

'It is so for me. I have shaped my life around not needing or wanting one.'

'And you do not find me a distraction?'

A dangerous question.

For here they stood in the kitchen, with no one around, her in a nightdress, and he in his suit, but with the collar and sleeves undone. They were half undressed between the two of them.

Thankfully, the child was between them.

'I am not the sort of woman who can afford distractions, Your Grace.'

'West.'

'Your Grace,' she said again, firmly. 'I must guard myself and my position.'

'But I do distract you.'

'What will I gain by admitting this?' she said, her voice dropping to a whisper. 'If I say I find you to be a handsome man, what will my reward be?'

She looked at him directly. A challenge.

His body was rioting. He wanted to tell her that the reward would be a night of pleasure in his bed.

He kept himself chained for this reason.

Because he knew what sort of destruction men caused when they embraced their own desires ahead of all else.

'Nothing. I understand what the consequences are for stepping off the path.'

'Then you understand I cannot.'

'And neither can I.'

'You aren't grieving your wife,' she said. 'There are mistresses you could have.'

'I am grieving what might have been.'

'I am sorry.'

She turned away, and then...looked back up at him. He felt his body going tight and hard when her gaze met his.

'You do not have to tell me you want me,' he said. 'Your eyes give you away.'

Colour mounted in her face, and this time it was anger. This time, she had not taken his words as light flirting. This time, he had overstepped.

'For all the good it does.' She looked down at the babe and then back to him. 'It is no different than...the challenge you face with this child. He's not yours, but there would be no glory in letting the world know. It would destroy Jane's reputation. Damage her own and make this child's life an impossibility. Such is my...'

'Your what?' He felt on edge. She was so bloody correct about the babe. And it lanced him that she was.

It was an impossible situation where the only possible course of action was to throw himself on his sword in private because it would spare them all a public execution.

He could not argue.

And that meant that she would be right about them as well, without her even speaking the words, he knew. Yet he wished to hear it all from her lips.

'My desire for you,' she whispered. 'It is impossible.'

It was his cue to back away. To leave. Not to push.

'You desire me?' he asked.

Dammit to hell, he felt like the rake he had never allowed himself to be.

But he *wanted*. He wanted to draw closer to her. He wanted to feel her soft hands on his body.

He was a man who had never struggled to keep himself in line. He was a man who had never once doubted what he ought to do. What he would do.

He was a man who believed in propriety above all else. Because of who could be hurt, and here she was pleading with him, telling him that it was impossible for her, and he should listen.

He knew. That was the problem.

He already knew, it was only that his resolve was going weak.

So damned weak.

'You make me feel…' She shook her head. 'It is not right. It isn't right. I have worked so hard to build myself a sterling reputation, something beyond reproach, and the moment that I walked into your home you questioned me. You doubted me, you…'

'I did.'

'You *saw* me,' she said, as if it was the worst offence that he could have ever devised against her.

'I did, and I do. I see your need for me and your eyes as well. Is it not reflected in mine?'

'Yes,' she whispered. She held the babe now like a shield. 'But the cost would be too great. For me, it would be too great.'

He knew she was correct. It would cost her. It wouldn't cost him anything—it couldn't. He was an unmarried man of great status, and he had nothing to lose by beginning an affair with her. She was his children's governess, but that was surmountable.

In society there might be talk, but talk of this kind was nothing to a duke. To admit his wife had birthed a bastard was one thing…but to dally with a woman in his household? Worthy of the sort of disapproval that rose in a whispered wave when he entered a room, but nothing more than that. Nothing more than whispers.

The only thing he had to lose was his honour. The centre of all that he'd made himself to be.

And already it was compromised. Already, with the way that he had failed Jane…

He had loved her. But his love was wrong.

Try as he might to be the caregiver, to do the best he could do, to be the best that he could be, he had failed her. She had sought out another man because he had not been able to love her in the way that she needed.

He could satisfy a woman. He knew that. He had satisfied her. But it hadn't been enough.

And he could feel it. He had always been able to feel it. It was as if his deepest emotions were buried beneath a rock fortress. And he had no idea how to let them out, let alone did he desire to let them out.

No. Because he did not know the line. He did not know how a man went from being passionate to being selfish. A pleasure-seeker. His father. His damned father.

That was what he did not know, and he did not know how to create those lines inside himself if they were not definitive, if they were not perfect in their delineations, and so he had done so.

He was the caregiver. The provider. He had chosen to become those things *relentlessly*.

But he had not been fun, and he had not been unrestrained, and he had not been her friend, and in the end perhaps that was all she had wanted. But he had never asked.

So perhaps it would not cost him. In the way that she meant. In society.

But it would cost everything that he had built himself to be.

And that was far too much.

'You may not understand this, but it is against everything that I believe in to take one of my household staff to bed. It would cost me. All that I am.'

She nodded slowly. 'I suppose I understand it in the same way as I understand what it means for myself.

'Yes, there would be a cost to me. But if no one were to ever know… I am not a lady. I am never going to marry. My reputation matters not, except as a governess. And no, no wife would hire me, young as I am, if they thought I was going to take their husband as a lover, but I told you from the beginning that if I wanted to be a mistress, I could be one. I have never had that desire.'

'You did say.'

'I did.'

And he felt like the last vestiges of the day, the warmth of the sun, and the smell of the earth, were slowly fading away.

As if reality was creeping in, cold and distant.

'There will be a new wet nurse soon.'

'Good,' she said. 'Good.'

'Why don't you take the child back to bed?'

'I am sorry,' she said. 'It must be very, very painful. This child. This reminder of the fact that your wife betrayed you.'

'I failed her. I failed her. And she died because of that.'

The words came out hard and blunt, and he had not meant to say them. He had a habit of that with her. Allowing things to fall out of his mouth that he would never normally.

'How?'

'If she was satisfied she would not have sought anyone else, would she?'

'She could have easily died giving birth to your child. And then you would blame yourself all the more. I think you are the sort of man who carries the responsibilities of the world on his shoulders. Your Grace...'

'West. We have spoken about desire for one another, why continue the charade?'

'Because I need it.' Her eyes filled with tears. 'I need to pretend. That we never spoke of this. That I never admitted that. To you or to myself. I need to forget that you ever touched me. And that I ever touched you. I need you to be the Duke. Because I cannot allow you to be West. And I must be Miss Smith. Please.'

Unbidden, a hard sound lodged itself in his throat.

'Do not beg me, Miss Smith, it is an act I find far too compelling.'

She did not shy away from that. Instead, she pushed harder.

'Please,' she said, beseeching.

'As you will it.'

She nodded, and he could see how much this cost her. Could see tears ready to fall.

She held the babe close and walked past him, out of the kitchen, and he let her go. He did not follow her.

Because following her would be an act of folly.

He stood there in the silence of this room that he never inhabited.

This room where he knew the location of nothing.

It was his house. And he never came in this room.

He laughed at the absurdity of it, and moved to brace himself on a table at the centre of the room.

The child could no longer go on without a name. It was as if speaking out loud the truth, that the babe was not his, had firmly placed his feet in reality.

He could not continue to keep the child without a name.

He had decided, by speaking this out loud to her. He had decided to keep the child, to name him, because everything that he had said to her was the truth. It would not do to expose Jane. It would not do to expose the child. What she had said in that regard was also true. And he was an innocent. West, on the other hand, was not.

He bore the shame and consequences for what had happened with his wife.

And so what he had said tonight, about the child not being his son… It would be the only time he said it.

For now, he had to become West's son.

In earnest.

He could only be thankful that he had hired her as a governess.

Because she would give the child what he needed. She would give the children what they needed. She would take care of them, and it was even more critical that he did not touch her for that reason.

His children had been through enough. And he had seen them today. Happy.

They'd even been happy in his presence.

That was because of her.

It was because of her.

He could not squander that.

She was what they needed.

She was, perhaps, what they all needed. And he could not destroy that for something so basic as sex.

His life had to be more than his desires. It always had been.

And so it would continue to be.

No matter how much he wanted her.

Or perhaps…it was time for him to change. The

thought was like a boulder shifting inside him. She was all these things to his children. He could see it. Why could he not be them? Why must his children be dependent on her to have a show of love?

He loved his children.

He had loved his wife and his inability to show it had destroyed her.

He would not destroy his children.

He would find it in him to fix this, to change this.

His father's iron hand would not extend itself to his children. His inability to find a path that was both steady and firm and loving was the fault of his father, and his children should not pay that price.

He did not know how. He would have to learn.

Perhaps Miss Smith was meant for him, in ways that went well beyond his desire for her.

Perhaps she could show him the way.

Chapter Fourteen

She awoke with a dull ache in her chest and in her head.

She had been up far too late with the bairn.

The bairn.

He was not West's child.

And when had she come to think of him as West? All the time.

No longer the Duke. But West.

At least she had not allowed herself to begin to think of him as his Christian name.

Even as she had that thought, *Samuel* whispered through her soul.

She would never speak it out loud. That would be an intimacy too far.

She remembered how he had touched her lips.

How he had stood there in the kitchen last night and spoke to her of desire.

And her whole body felt like it was ignited with need.

She had admitted that she desired him, for what little she knew of desire.

She knew about sex.

She knew about the most base, quick, clinical interpretation of it. But desire, that she knew nothing about.

It was so dangerous. He was so dangerous.

But the consequences for her would be…

Yes, she knew there were ways to prevent pregnancy, but there was always a risk. Look at his wife. If anything, it was a reminder. She was dead because she had given birth to the child of her lover.

Undoubtedly, she had not intended to conceive that child.

Why would she wish to compromise her position in society? She wouldn't. The woman was undoubtedly not an idiot.

She pressed her hand to her chest, felt her heart throbbing there for a moment. And she reminded herself that she was more than this.

She was Michael and Elizabeth's governess. She was… She was helping care for this infant.

And while it had felt like a deep wound at first, it was beginning to feel like balm.

She got up and got dressed. And ushered the children into the nursery.

'We'll go for another walk in the woods?' Elizabeth asked.

She had enjoyed that.

'I think we should.'

'Will Father join us this afternoon?' Michael asked, his voice hopeful.

And she decided that she was going to have to speak to the Duke at teatime.

There. She had thought of him correctly then. Being around his children helped.

It helped remind her that he was her employer. Not her...

She had begun to think of him as somebody that she knew. And that was not right.

He was not a friend.

And it was easy for her to convince herself that perhaps they knew one another. Perhaps she could speak to him with honesty.

She had certainly spoken with him more intimately than anyone else in her life.

She'd had trouble making friends at boarding school, for they had all known where she had come from.

If they had known that at the time she entered the classroom it had been four months since she had given birth, they would've ostracised her.

Thank God they had never found out.

They did their morning lessons, and when the children took their tea she found herself heading to the Duke's study.

He was not there.

'His Grace is shooting,' said Barrows.

'Thank you,' she said. 'Is he close?'

'Yes. Go on into the back garden and follow the sound.'

She went outside and heard the sound of a musket fire.

She headed down his direction, her skirts gathered in her hands. The ground was soft today, owing to a bit of rain from the previous night.

'Your Grace,' she said. She saw him there, wearing a navy-blue jacket.

And she wondered if it was because he had finally told the truth. It wasn't black, though it was close enough as to seem respectful. But she knew.

He lifted the gun and fired, the intensely masculine act sending a wash of heat through her.

What was wrong with her? Usually, she was not compelled by such things in the least.

But she had learned that there was no *usually* with him.

She was at the mercy of whatever his presence did to her body, and it was not anything that she could properly attribute.

He turned towards her, his expression fierce. 'Are the children with you?'

'No. I am allowing them to take their tea without me hovering over them. But… They were wondering if you would join us on a walk today. They had a wonderful time with you yesterday.'

He was devastating in the sunlight. His dark hair was tousled, as if he had run his fingers through it. His eyes were mesmerising. She could not look away from him. The brilliant square cut of his jaw. His broad shoulders. Broad chest.

She was so fascinated by his strength. By the physicality of him.

'You know, very few aristocrats enjoy the outdoors as much as you.'

'I doubt that's true. Many of them like a hound hunt.'

'I only meant,' she said, feeling her face grow hot, 'you seem a bit more physically active than most.'

'My brother and I spent a great deal of time outdoors when we were children. It was better that way.'

'You said your father was not a kind man.'

He shook his head. 'He was volatile.'

'I am sorry. I… I am sorry.'

'It is the way of things, is it not. You are a peasant girl from Scotland, and your father used his fists. I am a duke from England, and my father used his.'

And she had been raped in a field in Scotland. And she had been threatened by a man in a duke's home in England.

Men were devastatingly *the same*. The world over. Regardless of class, wealth, beauty or otherwise.

But he was not.

He was not, and she knew that. Definitively.

His children wanted to be around him and she…

She knew enough about men to have known from the moment that she saw him that he would never use his strength against her.

What she had not known was how much she would want to feel his strength around her.

Just thinking of that night in the study made her dizzy.

He had touched her lip. And it had sent her into a freefall. Had made her doubt everything about herself. Had made her question her deeply held beliefs.

He made her want to risk everything.

What would it feel like to have his hands gripping her hips?

What would it feel like if he was over her? In her?

'I would love to join you and the children,' he said.

'What changed?'

He shook his head. 'Perhaps I am trying to. You have made me see that I must change. I have tried… I have tried to be the provider. The steady hand. I want them to trust me. And to be able to depend on me. I don't know how to do that without staying at a distance from everyone and everything. Pulling my energy into appropriate categories, and making sure that I never make the mistake of… You must understand, my father wounded everyone around him by forcing us all to be players in a theatrical performance. All the world was his stage. And he was the lead. I have never wanted to hurt anyone. And yet I did. I hurt Jane. And you were right. The children have been hurt by all of this. Including the babe. And he does not deserve it. None of them deserve it.'

She felt dizzy. 'Your Grace,' she said. 'Are you quite certain you're well? Admitting that I am right?'

'More than that, I need you to teach me, Miss Smith.'

'It seems as if I already have.'

'I do wish you would call me West.'

She wished he would call her Mary. Both were impossible.

'And you know why I cannot.'

She wanted to. Absurdly, she found herself wanting to draw close to him now, rest her head on his chest, push her hand inside of that warm jacket and just breathe him in.

It was impossible. All of this was impossible.

But he was agreeing to take a walk with the children, so perhaps...

Perhaps being here had been worth it all along.

She was doing what she wanted for the children. Their father was going to be a bigger part of their lives now.

And that had to matter.

'I will accompany you back.'

She nodded slowly.

'I have decided that the child will be christened soon.'

She nodded and ignored the strange sensation in her stomach. 'Good.'

'I must think of a name.'

'What sort of name?'

'A good name.'

She laughed. 'And you don't know what a good name might be?'

'My wife named the other children.'

'I see.'

He'd had a wife.

For some reason, that hit her differently now.

His wife hadn't been faithful to him, no. But there had been a time when he'd been married to her in truth. They had children together.

The children she cared for.

He was older than her, she knew that. But more than that, he had lived an entire lifetime that she had never known. He had made vows to someone. Had promised himself to her, and he had kept those vows.

And now he was alone.

He was a mountain of a man. She had thought so from the moment she'd met him. And she would have thought that he might prefer to be alone, but now she didn't think so. She thought he didn't know how to be with anyone else, and she felt a kinship to that. She

had the children that she took care of. But she did not
have friends. She did not have family of her own. She
knew what it was to be isolated. To be lonely.

And in many ways she used that loneliness as a
shield. It protected her. And she felt as if it did much
the same thing for him.

They made their way into the house, not speaking.
There was a healthy amount of distance between them.
An entirely appropriate amount for the master of the
house and his children's governess.

And yet she felt tethered to him. It felt different.
And so did she.

When they went into the dining room, the children
were nearly through eating.

And they brightened when their father entered.

'You're coming with us, Father?' Michael asked.

'Of course. I wouldn't miss it.'

Their excitement was palpable, even though they
did not run to hug him. She could feel that they might
have. And that some day they would.

The walk was lovely. Though she did not linger behind with him as she had done during the first walk.

She was trying to remember why she was here.
Who he was, and what the purpose of their spending
time together was.

When they finished the walk, the children were
red-cheeked and exuberant.

'Children,' he said. 'Why don't you go to the nursery and play?'

'We have more school work to do,' said Elizabeth.

'I am pleased that you wish to do it. But I need to meet with Miss Smith.'

'Okay,' Elizabeth and Michael said together.

They scampered off before she could question what was happening.

'Your Grace…'

'Correct me if I'm wrong, but did you not miss your tea?'

'I did.'

'Then you should eat. The children will be fine for a while.'

He rang the bell, and one of the maids entered. 'Would you please fetch Miss Smith some sandwiches.'

'Yes, Your Grace,' the girl said, scampering off.

'You don't need to do that. I'm perfectly capable of waiting until dinner.'

'I do not wish you to be hungry,' he said.

Her throat went tight, and again she felt a shameless and shameful warmth between her legs.

Why should him offering food make her feel this way?

She had never been cared for.

And he did so. With authority.

It was very much the strangest thing.

And the most wonderful. The most lovely.

'Your Grace, I greatly appreciate that you see to my comfort.'

'I have told you. I care for what is mine.'

Mine. Mine.

The word that had echoed through her soul for all these years was lost.

Mine.

This was new.

This idea that someone might wish to keep her.

That she could belong to him.

He just means as a member of his household. Or perhaps even as a woman he wants to bed. And it is not something that you should take to heart.

No. But she ached. To be held by him.

To know all the other ways in which he might care for her.

She had been strong and independent and alone for so very long.

And even when she had been weak, surrounded by people, she had been alone. And suddenly, with him, she did not feel alone. She felt seen. Cared for.

She felt…

What a terrifying thing. To realise that she could want this.

She wasn't supposed to. She was supposed to be cured of it. She was supposed to be free. She was supposed to be happy. She was strong. She didn't need anyone.

But he was so enticing.

She remembered the way his hand had felt on her lip.

His strong hands. Hands that had held her when she was trembling.

She had never even allowed herself to tremble.

After she had risen from the bed when she had given birth to her son, she had never allowed herself to be weak again.

She was tired. She was so very tired. And the scones here were delicious. And somehow that made everything just a bit worse. Just a bit harder.

'You do not have to stay with me,' she said.

'I like to watch you eat. I like to watch you when you're being cared for.'

Trays of small sandwiches were served, along with scones and cream. Jam. Tea.

It was a lovely spread, the same that she had almost every day here.

'That is… It is a lovely thing. A kind thing. I thank you.'

He was watching her far too closely. 'It makes you uncomfortable.'

'It does not make me uncomfortable.'

'You seem like you might be.'

'It makes me want,' she said. The words came out

strange. 'That is all. No more. No less. It makes me want.'

'There is nothing that says you cannot have,' he said, his voice strong, hard.

'And yet you know there is. You know. You know what I cannot have.'

'I would make you forget everything.'

His voice was low, the promise so seductive. 'Your own name. Either of them.'

She wanted that. To forget who she was.

She wanted to know what he was offering her.

She wanted to feel it.

'I would make you wonder why you ever resisted this.'

'I will always know why,' she said. 'I will always know. Because I cannot afford to be naïve.' She looked up at him. And she was not refusing him. She did not know if she possessed the strength. But she would be honest. 'Women cannot afford to be naïve, West.' In her honesty, she would call him what she already did in her heart. 'Naïve women are destroyed in this life. I am well aware of what awaits a woman who puts a foot out of line. I will always remember why I made the choices I did. I will always know why they were necessary.'

'One thing is certain about you. You are strong,' he said.

'I've had to be.'

'I see. Take your tea. You do not have to come and meet me in my study tonight. But you are welcome.'

She understood the invitation. She knew precisely what it was.

If she came tonight, he would take it as agreement that she wished to be his lover.

God in heaven, but she did.

She was so tired. She was so tired of denying herself everything she wanted. Everything she craved.

She was so tired of being Spartan. Strong and independent. But what she wanted to do was brief. Rest.

She wanted to be held. And she didn't want to be alone.

You could risk everything for something you don't even like. You have no idea what will happen if a man touches you. If you wish to run from him. If you will hate the feel of his hands on your skin.

Except she knew she did not hate that. Not him.

Still, the idea of him moving over her, in her... It made her hot, and it made her heart beat too quickly.

'Thank you,' she said, for she knew she could not give an answer now. 'I will keep the invitation in mind.'

'Perhaps I will see you.'

'Perhaps.'

He laughed, and she let out a slow breath, and suddenly couldn't eat any of the glorious spread set before her.

What if she let him bed her? And it filled her with terror. What if she screamed and thrashed? What if it was the same as it had been the first time?

And would he take precautions with her? Would he ensure that he didn't get her with child?

If he did, she would have the bastard of a duke, and that was a damn sight better than the bastard of a rapist, that was sure.

But the shame…

There was the shame.

Slut.

Was she? To even consider this? Her mother had thought that she had the makeup of a whore.

And perhaps it was true.

Perhaps that was why she was entertaining this. Because in her very deepest parts, she was prone to this kind of thing. Maybe it had been obvious. Maybe that was why she had been chosen…

She wouldn't go tonight. She couldn't.

That denial made her want to weep.

But she had to take care of herself.

She had to remember. She was the only one who could really take care of herself. And no matter how tired she was, she had to remember. She had to keep moving.

She had to follow through.

There had been moments in her life when she had shared with others.

She'd had Penny.

But then she'd had to go. She could never return to Scotland.

Not when…

All she knew was that she wanted to lean into him.

To ask him to take care of everything.

To decide what she might teach, and when she needed rest.

Because he was much kinder to her than she was to herself.

And it just felt good. To rest.

It felt so indescribably good.

But could she allow herself this?

She had not been prepared for a duke. Not this duke. And yet it was the most singular connection she'd ever made in her life. She'd been hurt by men. Wounded. So deeply. And suddenly there was this man.

This man who made her feel like a woman. Like a woman who could want a man.

Maybe this wouldn't be her home for ever. It would've been nice.

But he had already been something to her no other man had ever been. Something like a friend.

And now she might find something else with him. Something she'd been sure had been taken from her for ever.

The ability to find pleasure at the hands of a man.

A piece of joy in the world, and she had always

thought that the girls who talked about such things were silly. The ones that spoke breathlessly of a wedding night, and what it might mean to know a man. She'd felt nothing but cynicism. Bitterness. Ash in her mouth. And she wanted to feel young again, and to enjoy being beautiful, rather than to see it only as a hindrance when it came to doing her job. She was never going to be able to do that, not in the real world, but perhaps with him. Just with him.

It was clear what he was offering. And it was not anything more or less than what she had told him she did not want when she had first arrived. Perhaps she should be disappointed in herself. For being no better than the wet nurse. For not heeding the cautionary tale she had been taught as a girl.

Except she didn't want to learn from that.

Suddenly, she was filled with an indescribable rage.

It had shaped her. It had made her safe, it was true. It was why she had learned how to use a knife, and it was why she had so successfully dealt with Pelham.

But she resented that. She resented that she'd had to change in response to a crime committed against her body.

She had done nothing wrong. She had done nothing wrong, and she did not deserve to carry that with her for the rest of her life.

In many ways, she didn't.

She was happy. She did love her life.

But this was a sizable thing that she had simply painted over and wiped from her mind. Made it into nothing. A canvas. Something she was never tempted to look at, nor paint on. But now she wanted to. In bold bright colours. Desire, sex, pleasure needed to be more than simply *there*, something that she could feel nothing about.

She wanted it to be *hers*.

And that was what had been lost. Above all else, and everything, her desire had not been hers for all these years.

She had submitted it to that travesty. Had sacrificed it upon the altar of safety. Of wishing to simply not think about what had happened.

And now she wanted to take it and make it something new. Something that was hers and hers alone.

And he was the man. He was the man to do that.

For she had not been looking for this, she had not asked for it.

And for the first time that felt like a glorious thing.

When he used his strength, it was only for good. When he gave commands, they were to care for everyone around him. She remembered his anger when she'd taken the children into the woods, it had not been a dangerous anger. It had been based on the need to keep what was his safe.

His orders were safe. His strength was safe.

Anyone under his hand was safe, and that was such a compelling and glorious thing to her.

Not since Penny and Lachlan had helped her had she been able to trust another person. She'd carried all her burdens on her own shoulders. Her well-being was hers and hers alone to manage.

He had given her tea. He cared for her comfort.

He would give her pleasure.

Her knowledge of what happened between men and women had been so badly distorted and she knew that only his strength was sufficient to rebuild it.

In this she would give him everything.

All the control.

She knew it was the only way, and more than that, something in her craved it.

She finished her tea, and then spent the rest of the day until bedtime a tangle of nerves.

Would she really do this?

Yes. She would. Because here she was going to be brave.

For herself.

And no one else.

She was going to grab hold of what she could have.

And relish the glory of the gift.

For she knew what it was like to be alone.

And tonight… She wouldn't be.

Chapter Fifteen

Would she come? And why did he feel so utterly beset by the question. He was a man, a man who could go out and get satisfaction whenever he wished. He could go to any brothel in London and have a whore. One who would do everything that he wanted and more. Why was he tempting himself—tempting himself to step outside the boundaries of what he knew was right and good?

They'd both spoken of fathers that had wounded them. That had wounded everyone around them. And was he any different? In pursuing this thing with her, was he any different?

He wanted what his flesh wanted, and he wanted it at the exclusion of all else.

She was his governess.

She had given something to the children, he could see it. A spark of happiness that had not been there before, and he had been there to witness it. Because she had given him something else. A connection.

She had brought him into a new place with the babe, and even if it was not one he wholly embraced yet, he was ready to make new steps.

Could he compromise all of it? She may well want to leave after this.

If she didn't come tonight, she might have packed her bags and run away.

The proposition to someone who he had this much power over… It was not who he was. It was not who he had ever been before.

Because he respected far too much the pain that a man in his position could cause. The ways in which the people around him felt they could not say no. And if she came to the door tonight, would that be the case?

Would it be because she did not think she could refuse him?

He would be sure. He would be certain.

Her position was not dependent upon her sharing her body with him. But he damn well wished she would.

He waited.

The clock ticked on.

He would deserve for her to not come.

It would be so wholly in the character of Miss Mary Smith.

To deny him. To not care that he was a duke, to not care that she earned her money at his behest.

Perhaps he shouldn't worry about her feeling forced

into anything. She argued with him with the freedom that no one else had ever evinced.

It was a truly spectacular thing.

But when he heard the knock on his door, his heart hit the front of his chest, and his cock hardened.

She had come.

'Come in.'

The door opened and Mary slipped inside, her face a bright shade of white.

'Your Grace…'

'Call me West.'

'West,' she said. 'I hope I have not misconstrued your invitation.'

'You know you have not,' he said.

And still he waited. There behind his desk, his correspondence untouched in front of him, he waited.

She moved into the room, and he was struck by her beauty.

He gave himself full permission to gaze upon her in a way he had not before.

He was playing a dangerous game.

No. He had gone beyond danger.

He had passed the threshold. He was, in fact, everything he had ever loathed.

He was a man disregarding the needs of somebody else, the potential concerns and cares that he should have for someone else, to seek his own pleasure.

He was a man who was far closer to his father than he had ever wished to be.

But he had failed. His method for living had failed him.

Jane was dead.

He had not protected her. He had not protected his children. He had not protected the babe that had fallen into his care.

So what good did it do? To deny himself? What good did it do?

What good could it ever do?

Perhaps those were the questions of a selfish man. Perhaps this was the justification of a man who simply wanted, above all else, to have what he desired. After two years of not knowing a woman's touch.

He would love to say that was why.

It was not so generic. If it were, he would've been at a brothel.

It was her.

She inflamed him. And his every base desire.

But she was not his wife, and she was not a lady.

She had come to his study, in spite of the fact that she knew full well what he was offering, and what he was not.

He did not even have to make a distinction. That this would only be an affair, that marriage could never be.

They both knew that. There was no use insulting

either of them by bringing it into the conversation. He was a duke.

She was a girl of absolutely no known parentage from Scotland.

There could be no question.

But she was here.

Because he had asked her to be.

Or maybe simply because she wanted to be, which was something he wanted to believe more than he wanted anything else.

More than he wanted his next breath.

He stood then, because he could not hold back any longer.

And he crossed the room to her, slowly.

As he had done many times since she had first come to work for him. But this time, there was no leash.

This time, they would not spar around what they both wanted.

This time, they would go right directly at it.

This time, they would lay claim to that which they truly desired.

He stood there. Looking at her.

She looked down, and one might have thought it was a genuflection. It nearly made him smile. Nearly. Except he was so hard he was quite past the point of smiling.

He put his finger beneath her chin and tilted her face upward.

'You came.'

'I did,' she said.

'Look at me,' he said. And on his command, those green eyes flashed up to connect with his. 'Very good. I am an exacting man. And my desires are no less exacting.'

'You are a duke. I would expect nothing less. And it is my job to serve your needs, is it not?'

'No. For if your needs are not served, there is no point in the coupling. I desire your pleasure.'

'I have a feeling it shall be easy for me to give that to you.'

He could see the pulse at the base of her neck beating rapidly.

'We shall see. I need you to understand that your job is not in jeopardy if you leave this room right now. What I need from you, what I desire from you, is capitulation. Absolute and total. It cannot be forced, and it cannot be under duress.'

Her eyes widened. 'It never occurred to me. Perhaps a woman such as myself, a woman who has spent her entire life protecting herself, and her work, should have thought of this above anything else, but I did not. In any other household, I would have. But I never once thought that if I did not come tonight you would relieve me of my position. Not once. I trust you. And if I did not I wouldn't be here. So whatever your exacting desires entail, I am here. For them. For you.'

'Good. You must tell me if ever something falls outside of your comfort. You must. You understand me?'

She nodded. 'Yes. I do. Your Grace.'

And this time *Your Grace* wound through him like an aphrodisiac, igniting his lust. Inflaming his need. It was sensual. The closest he was going to get to genuflecting, he imagined.

And it was exactly what he needed.

She was exactly what he needed. He moved his hand to cup her cheek, and slid his thumb over her cheekbone. He would take it slow.

He would.

He would act out his every fantasy with her.

She was his.

And there was no need to speak of what it was, and what it could not be. He would not insult her by making it clear he could not offer marriage, for she knew that already. She was a smart woman. He was a duke, and she was a woman of unknown parentage from Scotland.

She knew.

As well as he did. What this could be, and what it could not be.

But here, between them, and in his bedroom, it would be everything.

He had been married.

He had loved his wife, and it had not been enough.

He had his heir, he had his way, and by default he

even had a spare. The child was not his in blood, the world would never know that.

He had no need to ever marry again.

And he would not.

But he would have this. With her.

But there could only be this one moment before they kissed.

Where they both knew that it would happen, and yet it had not yet.

And he aimed to enjoy it. To let it draw out.

She began to tremble beneath his hand, and he felt the same harsh kick of desire work through his own body.

'Beautiful,' he whispered, his voice rough. Gruff.

He moved his thumb over her lip. And this time, he would not pull away.

He had this one moment. This single solitary moment of sanity before they touched and this spark became a conflagration. He knew that.

And so he wished to live in it.

Anticipation was part of desire, at least he had always thought so. But this was different. Remarkably different to anything that he had ever experienced before.

With his wife, sex had been a dutiful and respectful act.

He had found pleasure in it, in her, but he had been bound. By propriety.

He had been restrained in his actions with her, because it was what love meant.

As he understood it, love was first and foremost about ensuring that your own needs were never put above others'.

He had been respectful. He had been caring in regard to her pleasure. And methodical in figuring out the ways in which she could reach her peak. He was a man, and for him an orgasm was as simple as a timed number of strokes.

Yes, there were other things he enjoyed, but it was much like food. A man might like a five-course meal but he did not need it to survive.

Then with harlots, there was no anticipation. It wasn't a game. It was a transaction. He did not linger in moments of anticipation. Wondering what it would be like when their lips finally met. No.

But here, now, he did. Relished this space where need was so very raw. So very real.

And what was to come would be as decadent as they decided it to be. It would not be dictated solely by his tastes, but by hers as well.

And that was a new sensation.

For in a business transaction the only needs that truly mattered were his. It did not matter that he said he cared for the pleasure of the woman he was with, his needs were the ones that were discussed. His specific tastes were outlined. Agreed to.

And when it came to Jane it had been, in essence, about her, and yet also about the title. About everything he wished to be while fully inhabiting his space as the Duke. As her husband.

But then her pink tongue darted up to touch her upper lip, and he was lost.

He growled, drawing her body forward, crushing her breasts to his chest. She let out a short, shocked moan—pleasure, he could see it on her face. In the rising colour of her skin.

He traced the line of her jaw, to the centre of her chin, and then around the other side, and she let her head fall back. Then he let his hand drift down and made a cage for her throat with his palm. She held still, like prey in the jaws of a predator.

And a kick of desire raced through his body. Made him feel powerful. Desired.

For she could fight him if she wished, and she didn't.

She was surrendering.

It was in every line of her body. The set of her shoulders, the way that her beautiful mouth went soft.

He moved his hand upward again, and held her face steady as he leaned in and pressed his mouth to hers.

And the world around them began to burn.

Chapter Sixteen

This was unlike anything she had ever imagined. She had never imagined it, that was the problem, perhaps. But she had never been kissed. And the press of his firm mouth to hers was something that went quite beyond the reaches of her previous imaginings.

He smelled so good. Soap and his skin and West.

This man who meant something to her that was quite beyond anything.

His mouth was certain, his lips knowing as he parted them, and touched the tip of his tongue to hers.

Her knees went weak, soft, and she found herself sagging against him. And his firm grip held her up.

The way that he used his strength to guide her, to keep her from falling, it was more intoxicating than anything ever could be.

And she was lit up from within.

A pulse pounded between her thighs, and she knew full well what it meant. That whatever her trepidation, whatever her fears, she wanted him. She wanted him there.

She wanted to weep with the triumph of that.

With the glory of this need.

She wanted to howl with pleasure.

God save her, she was ignited.

He kissed her, deeper, longer, harder.

Locked onto her mouth and made her feel weak and strong all at once.

'Kiss me,' he growled.

And she wrapped her arms around his neck, clinging to him. The press of her breasts against the firm wall of his chest was incredible. He was so hot. So strong. And that strength would've frightened her before.

And now she loved it. Wished to play with it. With the bonds of it. How far he might carry her, how intensely he might push them both.

He kissed her, and they grew breathless. Hot.

He released his hold on her face and backed her up against the bookshelf, and then he gripped her wrists, pushing them up over her head and pinning her there.

She was trapped. Between him and the wall.

And she had been in this exact position only days ago, and she had used a knife to defend herself. But she was not afraid now.

Not of him.

And she felt wild. Reckless. Filled with the kind of

freedom that she would never be able to describe, not even to herself. Not in words.

For this was part of her. A part of her restored, reclaimed.

Hers.

His strength was testing her own, and it was a glorious thing.

To have been absent of this feeling all these years, and to be strong in it now, was a gift that she had never yet imagined.

Oh, how she loved it.

She arched against him, pressing her breasts more firmly against him, and he moved his free hand to cup her breasts, his thumb moving over one tightened bud there, and drawing a raw cry from her lips.

He kissed her. The scrape of his whiskers, grown longer from the day, a delicious friction against her skin.

And she thought, she really did, that she might be able to languish in this kiss for the rest of eternity.

Whatever came next didn't matter. There was this. And it was everything.

He parted her mouth even wider, and licked her tongue, going deep, consuming her. And it was such a sensual act. It had nothing to do with that selfish, hideous thing she had experienced all those years ago. He wasn't taking from her. He was giving to her. Even as he was all man, he was giving.

Even as his grip was punishing and bruising, it was all within a boundary that cared for her response.

That cherished it.

When she let out little moans of desire he made short sounds of praise in the back of his throat.

And then he began to verbalise that praise. 'Good girl,' he whispered against her ear as he kissed along her jaw, down her neck. To the tender swell of her bosom over her chemise. 'You please me.'

It made her want to cry, foolishly, ridiculously, she could not say why.

Except she could not remember the last time anyone had been pleased with her, and certainly not in such a fashion.

She had been told that her body was bad. That her desires would have been wrong, had she ever had them.

That she had somehow been bred for the disaster that had befallen her, and that there was something rotten within her, but he said that she was good.

He praised her kissing him, pressing her body to his.

For moving her hands so that they bracketed his face, and holding him steady as she experimented with taking the lead in their kiss.

His breathing was harsh, his heart raging in his chest.

'Not here,' he said, his voice rough. 'To my room.'

'We will be seen,' she said, the words punctuated by kisses, for she could not separate herself from him entirely.

'We will not. There is a way.'

He moved her away from the bookshelf, where he knew he would find it. A throwback from his father, who had been fond of drama, and of trying to get away with torrid affairs. A back passage into his bedchamber from his study was a most convenient tool. 'I have never used it for this purpose. I feel it is important you know that.'

She nodded, feeling suddenly adrift. Because of course he'd had lovers. He had a wife. But surely there had been others.

He gripped her chin, making her look at him. 'There was never another woman for me in this house. Only my wife. And we did not engage in clandestine sessions in my study.'

'I see.' She nodded.

'I wish that you *would* see. You would understand that this is extremely irregular behaviour for me.'

'And for me as well.'

He kissed her again, all that consuming her, and then released her, taking her hand to lead her down the concealed door that led to the hidden stairs.

She did not know how long they walked, for it was very dark. And she lost all sense of time. Her heart was pounding so hard it was making her dizzy, and the anticipation in her body was building. And building.

They stopped at a door, and he pushed it open, allowing them entrance into the opulent bedchamber.

There was already a fire lit in preparation for his arrival, casting an orange glow on the room. Aided by the illuminated candelabras that were placed about the room.

The bed was large and stately, with navy-blue curtains hanging around the fourposter frame.

There was a writing desk in here as well, and the quill and paper set just so.

It was neat and orderly, and absolutely everything she would have imagined his chamber might be.

But it was the bed that dominated her thoughts.

For the bed was why they were here.

He kissed her again, and then picked her up off the ground, his mouth fastened to hers as he laid her down at the centre of the massive mattress.

She sighed, arching up against him, and she was blessedly relieved to find that this, even this, did not bring about any bad feelings.

His body over hers felt right.

Because his strength was not a weapon.

His muscles were not being used for force.

And the hard rod that she felt in his breeches would not be used as a battering ram.

And she would not be used as an object. He had proven that already.

Sufficiently. Gloriously.

The kissing was feverish again, their breath mingling together, creating something near enough to a symphony.

'Please tell me,' he rasped, kissing down her throat, 'that you are not a maid.'

Something inside of her burst like a firecracker.

Because somehow she had thought, she had *always* thought, that if this question was asked of her, the answer she would have to give would be an indictment of her character.

But she could hear it in his voice, in the way that he had said that. He wanted the answer to be *no*.

Here, her lack of virginity was not a black mark on her character. It was permission.

'No,' she whispered.

'Thank Christ,' he ground out, tearing her chemise, pulling it down and exposing her breasts.

'I… I don't have many of those.'

'I will get you more. Whatever you need. Whatever you want.'

He made promises to her, even as he used his brute strength to push her down, down all the way, to expose her breasts.

It was rough. There was no finesse.

And yet it was still as far away from what had happened to her all that time ago as anything could be.

Her nipples were tight, begging for his attention.

Begging for his touch.

Her entire body was crying out for release.

'So lovely,' he said, his voice hard. 'Such beauty.' He reached up to palm her breast, her soft, pale skin a contrast against that dark, rough hand of his.

He pinched her, and a short cry rose up in her throat.

He was not gentle.

She did not want him to be.

For this was not to be a watercolour on that blank canvas of her soul.

It was to be bold. Great daubs of paint, vivid lines, and she was standing in his strength, and in hers.

And she was being renewed.

A kiss at a time.

With every touch of his callused hand over her untried skin.

Then he lowered his head, sucking one nipple deep into his mouth, his teeth scraping along that sensitised flesh.

She let her head fall back, a raw cry escaping.

'Good?'

'Yes,' she affirmed.

'More?'

And she knew then. Whatever she wanted, he would give her.

He was dominant. Strong. But when he'd said that he needed her absolute surrender, he had meant it.

And he was going to ensure, every step of the way, that whatever he did she wanted.

It was like the last vestiges of her resistance crumbled away. That very last bit of fear.

There was nothing to fear with him. And this was the glory of great strength in a good man.

It made her want to cry.

For this was something she had never yet seen.

But it existed.

Jane had been a fool. To have sought out another man when she had this one.

It was a strange thing to think of his wife.

And yet she could not help herself.

For what woman would trade anything, anything at all, for this man?

How could she surrender her life? How?

It made no sense.

This was everything real and fantastic that she had never dared believe in.

He was like a dragon. Mystical and great in his beauty. A terror that was hers and only hers.

That was real for her.

He sat her up and released her dress the rest of the way, pulling it completely from her body, along with her undergarments. Her stockings. And he left her bare to his gaze.

He was still clothed, a position of power that would have frightened her before, but now filled her with a delicious sense of anticipation.

He took off his jacket and slung it across a chair near the bed. Then he loosened his cravat.

He was left in a waistcoat and his white shirt, his snug-fitting black breeches.

Close, he was formidable. Beautiful.

And she knew that she should feel like a virgin sacrifice. But the glory was, she was not a virgin. Nor was she sacrificing herself here, on the altar of his need. No.

She was joyously claiming it.

Happily embracing it.

And if the sacrifice tied herself to the stone, then it wasn't a sacrifice at all, was it?

The power was with her, just as much as him.

She watched as his eyes grew hungry, and she had run from that expression in men's eyes all these years.

She could not afford their hunger.

The cost was too great.

And now she luxuriated in it. Opened herself up to it. She found her legs relaxing, her thighs opening.

And the sound he made was definitely that of a dragon.

'Yes,' he said, moving to slowly unbutton his waistcoat. 'Part your legs for me. Show me. How wet and glistening you are.'

She was wet. She ached.

The sensation was unfamiliar, except when it came to him. For she had that sensation when thoughts of him had spiralled out of control.

It would ease his passage, she knew that.

She was thankful for it.

And she did exactly as she was instructed.

'Good. Touch yourself. As you like.'

She froze. She had no idea how she liked to be touched. And the idea of putting her own hands on her slick flesh seemed a heresy.

'Do as I command you,' he said, undoing his sleeves. Moving to his white shirt and opening it, showing her his well-muscled chest, and the hair that covered it, which fascinated her.

Her mouth was dry with need, and she knew that she could ill afford to disobey him.

More than that, she did not wish to disobey him.

So slowly, very slowly, she sneaked her fingers between her legs and touched herself, finding a pleasure there that was like a streak of lightning through a night sky.

She was so wet it was nearly an embarrassment, and yet she did not see why she should be. He was looking at her with open desire. His need was naked, even though he was not.

And so she began to stroke herself, pursuing more and more of that sensation. Inviting in a feeling that she had kept the door firmly closed on for all these years.

For any time she had been lying in bed at night and felt errant desire roll through her, she had denied it.

She had never encouraged it. Never touched herself.

Never continued down that path, because it was a path that led only to ruin.

And now she was running towards ruin. Towards him.

'Yes,' he said, his breath hissing through his teeth.

He began to undo the falls on his breeches, kicking his boots off as he did.

And he exposed himself to her.

He was… He was beautiful. But far too big. Thick and imposing, even as he was a sincere work of art.

She had never seen a naked man.

And his every line, every cord of muscle, every hard delineation, was a triumph in divine artistry. His thighs were large and heavily muscled, his masculine member hanging heavy between them. There were deep grooves cut into that place just above his member, and his stomach was entirely ridged, his chest deep and broad.

Her mouth went dry, and between her thighs she only grew wetter.

It felt easy now to stroke herself, to find her pleasure.

He wrapped his own fists around his masculinity, and she found herself staring at him with rapt focus.

It was such a gift, to be able to look at him like this. To allow her gaze to take ownership of each and every part of him. Education, she had always found, helped her with any fear or heartbreak or horror she had yet endured.

And it was like he was giving her a moment.

To familiarise herself with the feelings. To control them for a moment.

To find her way with a tour of his body.

He did not know it, but he was granting her the opportunity to have everything she needed from this encounter, and she wished to jump up off the bed and wrap her arms around him, kiss his face for it.

And in fact she didn't see why she could not. She moved then, getting up to her knees and moving to the end of the mattress, wrapping her arms around him and pulling her to him, her bare breasts brushing his chest. She kissed his cheek, down his jaw, and to the corner of his mouth.

He let out a sound that could best be described as feral. Her hand began to move down his chest and he gripped her wrist, stilling her movement.

'No. This will be over before it begins, and I have a need to enjoy myself. To draw this out.'

'Thank you,' she whispered.

'For?'

'For you. For your...'

Her cheeks felt hot.

She had indeed been on the verge of thanking him for that most masculine part of him. And he seemed to know exactly what she'd meant to say.

'We will come back to that,' he said. 'Because I will want to hear it from your lips, darling girl.'

And then she found herself being pushed roughly back onto the bed.

Pinned to the soft mattress. But what she expected him to do was… Not what he did.

He did not rise up and thrust into her. Rather, he gripped her hips and pulled her towards his mouth, his tongue unerringly finding the place where she had just been stroking herself.

She lifted her hips up off the mattress. 'Your Grace.'

'West,' he growled against her slick flesh.

He pinned her there, feasting on her as if she were a delicacy.

And her thoughts went every which way, billiard balls bouncing off the edges of the table. Going every which way.

All she could do was cling to his shoulders.

All she could do was hold tightly to him.

She cried out as he held her tightly, then clasped his fingers over the low, soft part of her stomach, preventing her from struggling against him as he licked yet more deeply into her.

'West,' she whimpered, putting her hand on the

back of his head, pushing her fingers through his hair and clinging tightly to him.

Her sounds became animal-like.

This was pleasure beyond anything that she had thought might exist on this earth.

For her, the most glorious thing of all had been a warm bath. A warm bath and cake. And this was better than either of those things.

It was better than hot tea after a rainstorm. It was better than having a full belly every day when she went to sleep, something she had never once taken for granted.

It was better than anything she had ever experienced. It was like she was being released from her skin, free, in a way that she had never been before.

This was art.

This was living.

This was who she was. And free.

And when she began to reach for this impossible thing, something she could not name, it was as if everything inside of her was wound tight.

And she was certain that it had to break soon or she would.

'West,' she said, his name like a prayer.

West. West.

A new echo for her soul.

West.

And then he shifted, putting his hand between her

thighs to join his tongue. He pushed two fingers inside of her, and it was like the world broke apart. All that was real shattering into illusion, as a bright white light broke through and showed her what was new. What was real.

An ever pulsing wave of satisfaction that rolled through her entire being, her internal muscles clenched tight around his finger.

This was why.

This was why people upended their lives for a chance at this.

It was why women walked down dark garden paths. It was why they married.

This.

This powerful, wretched need that outstripped anything she had ever before known.

It was this.

In all its brilliant, uncivilised glory.

For they, all of them, walked around using titles, bowing, curtsying. And in the dark, without their clothes, this was what they were. This was what they wanted.

And she had never felt more real than she did right now.

He kissed his way up her body, and then his hand was around her throat again.

He wrapped his other arm around her waist and

adjusted her roughly, moved her up the bed, her head coming to rest on the pillow.

His touch was rough, but it was to put her on something more comfortable.

His hold was possessive, but never to wound.

His strength was overwhelming, but never there to simply be overpowering.

And then he parted her thighs, his movements firm and decisive, as he pushed his fingers between her legs and stroked her, pushing two inside of her and watching as he did so.

She felt a vague hint of shame roll through her.

That she was allowing this.

That she was relishing it.

And then she banished the shame, because had she not been under the banner of it long enough? She would be under her own banner now.

And all the world, that had only sought to hurt her, and then to blame her for the hurt that it had caused, could go to hell. With the very devil.

She returned her focus back to him.

'Are you ready for me?'

She could only nod.

And then he moved himself into position, hooking one arm around her thigh and drawing her down to him, before positioning that blunt, wide head of his arousal at her entrance.

Then he flexed his hips forward. There was a bit of pain.

Not a fresh, tearing pain, for none of her innocence remained. But these muscles were in disuse. And she had given birth, and healed again, and since then there had been nothing. No one.

She gritted her teeth and found that there was a strange sort of satisfaction in the pain.

She could not have explained it if asked.

But she was grounded in the moment because of it. In him.

And then he pulled her down hard, impaling her entirely on his length. A real growl escaped her lips, at the same time as one escaped his.

What were they? They were like the beasts in the forest around Attingham.

They were hardly human in that moment.

He gripped the back of her head, pulling her up off the mattress and pressing her forehead against his. 'Yes,' he said.

She nodded, unsure of what she was agreeing to, only knowing that she did.

He began to move, his thrusts animalistic, rough and glorious. She was slick with need.

She was ready for him.

She wanted him.

And this was what it was supposed to be.

Strength it gave.

Strength that fed your soul.

That stoked desire.

It took nothing.

Over and over again, he filled her.

One hand holding firmly to her hip, the other on her head, his fingers gripping her hair tight.

And she had been so focused on what it meant for her, that she had not paused to think what it meant for him.

This man who was so perfectly composed in all ways. To be a beast like this.

And yes, she took for granted that he had done this before, but this was… A side of him. Something that she had never seen.

There was a thrill to that. To the fact that she knew this man with clothes on. Knew him as Your Grace. Knew him behind his desk.

But she knew him as a man who had looked lost in the kitchen that day, as she had fed the bairn that wasn't his but that he was forced to claim as his own.

That she had never seen him, naked and raw, and he was in her body, seeking his own pleasure even as he gave out hers.

'West,' she said, broken.

And he began to drive into her harder, pushing her up the mattress, her head coming into contact with the headboard behind her.

Over and over again, with each and every thrust.

And it was perfect.

'Tell me,' he growled, 'tell me that you are mine.'

'I'm yours, Your Grace,' she said, the words broken, but no less true for it.

'Good girl.'

And that broke something inside of her, a second peak forming inside of her, but this one was different.

It started deep and radiated outward.

It went on and on, and the feel of him, like iron inside of her as her need pulsed was unending, destructive. Perfection.

And then, suddenly, his movements became more intense.

He wrapped his hand around her throat again, holding her, tightening his grip as his thrusts became erratic.

He held her very life in his hand, and she could trust him with it. And it was like a key had turned in a lock inside of her soul, and she was free.

In ways she had never known she was captive.

'West,' she whispered.

And suddenly he moved away from her and groaned harshly as he spilled himself onto the bed sheets.

And she realised with a rush of gratitude just exactly what he had done.

Foolish girl.

She wanted to cry.

She had been so careful, for all this time, for all these years, and she had lost herself.

And even in this, he had cared for her.

She wrapped her arms around his neck and held herself against him. 'Thank you,' she whispered. 'Thank you.'

'For what?' he asked, pulling away and cupping her cheek. 'For…'

'For spilling outside of me. Thank you.'

He nodded slowly. She leaned back against the pillow, tears gathering in her eyes.

'You said you were not a maid,' he said.

'I was not.'

'It has been a long time,' he said. It was not a question.

She nodded. 'It has been.'

The room felt like it was spinning. Or maybe it was her.

She couldn't be sure. She wasn't certain she would ever be sure of anything again.

'How long?'

She didn't have to count. She knew exactly how long.

'Nine years.'

He sat up. His movements suddenly harsh.

'You were a child.'

She nodded.

Her defences were obliterated by him. She had no ability to keep this inside, nor even the desire.

It was like all shame had been lifted from her. And perhaps it was foolish. But here they were. She was a governess in his house, and they had lain together. He'd said that he wanted to know her. And so now he could.

'I was.'

'You did not lie with a man. You were raped.'

She nodded. 'Yes.'

'That is why you carry a knife.'

'Yes,' she said, her throat tightening, going aching and painful.

'I asked you if there was a man in Scotland and you became upset.'

'Yes. I did. Because in the strictest sense, there was a man in Scotland. A man who did something to me that changed everything.'

A tear slid down her cheek, and it was the strangest thing, because she was not sad. It was only that everything felt so large, and so undeniable now.

She had never spoken of this. Not to anybody. Not really.

She hadn't had to when Penny had found her.

'My name is Mary McLaren. Of Clan McKenzie. When I was thirteen I was walking home from collecting food in the forest. For my siblings. There was a man, a man who believed himself to be above reproach. To be above any sort of consequence. He stole me and pushed me into the back of the houses. He pushed me down into the mud, and what happened was… It was nothing like this. It was nothing…'

'I was rough with you,' he said.

She nodded. 'Only to the degree that I encouraged you to be. You gave me power. And you gave me a choice.'

She could see that he was stricken.

'I had a choice,' she reiterated. 'I never once thought that you would release me from my job if I didn't come to your study tonight. Don't you understand? I have known how men are since I was far too young. Do you not see why I thought it was so important that your children understood…? I have known since I was a child exactly what happens when a man wants something and feels that he should be allowed to take it. I have known what mystery occurs between men and women, and I thought that I knew everything. But I was wrong. What happened to me is not like this. What happened to me is the difference between a sword fight and a ballet.'

'Mary,' he said, his voice rough, 'I wish you would've told me before.'

'So you could have treated me with more care? No. I did not wish this to be about your feelings. It was about mine.' She looked down at the coverlet, at the embroidery on it. 'I spent my whole life without choice. Without a family who cared for me. I had no dreams. I knew nothing of the outside world. I knew only poverty and hunger and neglect. And then a man took my body like it was his, he used me. He took away the only thing I had that was *mine*.'

'But you're here.'

'I am here. I made more of myself. I found out I had much more than what had been taken, and I learned what I wanted, what I could be. And that it had nothing to do with my mother or my father, with that man who hurt me.' A tear slipped down her cheek and she wiped it away. 'I never wanted a man. In all the years since. But I wanted you. And I… I wanted it to be the way I desired it. I wanted it to be for me. Because that was one thing I had not reclaimed. And I needed to. On my own terms.'

He reached out and took her chin in his hand, tilted her face up to him. 'I was told there were acts a gentleman was not to visit on a lady. I gave into temptation with you.'

'You gave me what I wanted. I will tell you the truth now, everything. But I wanted to be with you and not have my past in your mind. It was years ago for me. An old wound. Had I told you beforehand it would have affected everything.'

He nodded slowly. 'Yes.'

'I would have worried it changed how you saw me.

How you felt. What you did. I felt I was owed a night without worry.'

'You were,' he said gravely. 'You are.'

They said nothing for a long moment. And she knew that she should tell him.

'I was… He got me with child.'

She could see that he was struggling with violence.

'I almost died,' she said softly. 'Very nearly I did.'

'Mary…'

'And that is why it was so difficult for me to hold the bairn.' Even without her brogue, these familiar words were often easier when her heart was sore. 'You told me why you struggled, and I needed to tell you. I needed you to know. It was not a lack of care. Never. It's only that I never held my own son.' She put her hand over her mouth. 'My son. I have never spoken those words out loud.'

'What became of the child?'

She took a breath, as if it could fortify her. As if it could hold back her tears.

'Never has a girl who endured so many terrible things been given such a great gift. The leader of my clan is raising him as his own. As his heir. My son is going to be the leader of our clan. He has been given everything.' She looked down. 'I did not name him. I do not know his name now.'

Both of them had nameless babies in their lives. For

wholly different reasons and yet the pain felt similarly impossible.

'They do not write to you?'

'I asked them not to. I wanted him to have a new life, and I wanted one as well. I did not want either of us to be tied to the other. We are, of course.' She tried to smile. 'The idea that we wouldn't be was the desperate hope of a thirteen-year-old girl who wanted to forget. But you cannot forget. Not something like that.'

'Do you think you might write and learn of him some day?'

'He is not mine. His life is his own. Whatever he wishes, that is what I want. Who knows what they will tell him? Some day... I would like to see him some day. But only when I can be sure I am not robbing him of anything. His birthright, his status in the clan. His security. It is all complicated, you see.'

He nodded. 'I am familiar with such complications.'

'Yes, indeed. If Jane's baby is discovered to be a bastard, what becomes of him? They know the Laird's wife didn't give birth to my bairn, but the circumstances behind his birth aren't known widely. I was no one and nothing. It might harm him to know the truth.'

Part of her did wish, now, to know.

But never at his expense.

'How did you then come to be under the care of the Duke of Kendal?'

'The Duke of Kendal was engaged to Lady Penelope Hastings. Lady Penelope was taken, as payment for a debt owed by her father. She was taken by Lachlan Bain, the McKenzie. She and Lachlan married and… Even though it created a scandal when Kendal's engagement was broken…'

'I remember that,' he said. 'Only vaguely.'

'Yes. The engagement was broken, and then he married his ward.'

'Of course.'

'And because of that, because the broken engagement led him to his beloved wife, when Penny wrote to him and asked if they could speak well of me, offer me their sponsorship, he agreed. I declined to have a season because…'

'You did not wish to marry.'

She shook her head. 'No. For very clear reasons, I did not wish to marry. But they helped see me through school, and they helped me get my first position as governess.'

'How did you find the fortitude within yourself to do these things? I was handed an education. Money. Power. You had none of it, and yet you stood up from that mud, and you never looked back towards it.'

'I look back plenty enough. There were reasons I knew how to use a knife.'

'And God damn the men that make it necessary for you to do so. They prove you correct. Men like my father.' His voice had gone very rough. 'Do you see,

I had struggles. I could not overcome them, not with a fraction of the grace that you have shown here. You are a miracle, Mary Smith. Mary McLaren.'

And for the first time that name did not feel haunted.

It did not feel like it was reaching out to try and strangle her. Because it didn't carry a dark secret. He knew. He knew and, just like in his study with Pelham, he did not blame her.

'My mother said that I was a whore. In my soul. And that he was a man who could sense that. That I had brought it on myself. I did sometimes wonder if that was true. When Pelham singled me out. And then when… When I came to work for you and I desired you so… I thought only a harlot could want such things.'

He was silent for a moment, his hands tracing shapes along her bare hips. And then he spoke.

'Do you know that in wolf packs there is a hierarchy. And the leader hunts, for the protection of the pack. For food. They have no interest in people, because there is any number of better game for their consumption. When you hear of wolves attacking men, it is because one is weak. Sick. Because it has been cast out of the pack. And if a wolf ever attacks a human, it is not about the human, but about what is sick inside the wolf. He was nothing more than a sick wolf. With something irretrievably damaged within him that makes it impossible for him to behave in a way that is right or intended.'

It was as if something truly heavy had been lifted from her chest, from her shoulders.

She had come to a place where she had not believed that she was the broken one, but the way that he had stated that. So bluntly, so clearly. So undeniably.

The damage was not within her. And it never had been.

The damage was his.

'I want to make it quite clear that he is a waste of oxygen and of effort to even speak of. But what did become of him?'

'Lachlan killed him. He made it clear there was no room for those sorts of actions within the clan. He set an example. That they would all know.'

'He sounds like a good man. A man to be respected.'

'He is. You will stand shoulder to shoulder with him.'

She could see that he was taken aback by that. That he did not quite know what to say.

'Thank you,' she said.

'For?'

'You have listened to me. And offered no judgement. My deepest fear is not lying with a man. It was someone other than my mother knowing this truth and finding me to blame as well. You have given me something new.'

'Stay with me,' he said.

'I cannot. The servants…'

'You will go out the back passage when necessary. Stay with me until the early hours.'

And she found herself unable to do anything more. Because he was there. And he was strong and she could rest. Against that strength, in his arms.

And nothing in the whole world had ever felt so glorious.

She had not been prepared for the Duke.

But she was very glad to have found her way to him.

He was up at first light, and Mary was already gone. He'd known she had to leave, but his bed already felt empty without her. A foolish thought. He and Jane had never shared a bed with one another for the whole night.

He found he wished he could share with her. Hold her. Wake up with her.

He got up and dressed himself, not waiting for his valet.

There was something about her story that created a deep shift within him. That made him question things.

He walked to the children's wing, and to the nursery. The babe wasn't crying.

But he still found himself walking into the nursery. It was unoccupied at the moment, as they had found a new wet nurse, but she would not be here until midday.

He went into the room and looked down at the little body.

He could see Jane. Bleeding and pale, the bairn screaming, covered in her blood, lying at the foot of the bed.

The doctor working feverishly to try and save her. *'Your Grace. Hold the child.'*

He hadn't been able to bring himself to do it. He had not.

For… It was not his.

And yet who else would claim this child? No one. He thought about Lachlan, the leader of her clan, who had taken a child conceived in hateful circumstances. He had meted out justice. Judgement.

And it had been brutal. And yet when it came to his treatment of the babe, he had been compassionate. Beyond compassionate.

He reached down into the cradle and picked up the sleeping child. 'Lachlan,' he said, testing the name. It was Scottish, unforgivably so, but he was a duke. So in all likelihood the name would be seen as an interesting eccentricity.

Lachlan.

That was what he would name the child. Lachlan Samuel. His own name. Jane had not given his own name to their son. And yet he felt that it would make a strong tie between them, and now he wanted to do so. He wanted to make that claim.

Because a man had been there for Mary when she had needed him most, and he had come alongside a helpless child. And he felt… He felt that he needed to do the same here.

He held the child close, and he felt something soften inside of him.

'You are my son,' he said.

Because he had been a wall. He had been steady. He had been stable, but all of that kept what needed to spill over back as well.

He needed kindness here. A compassion that he had not felt.

How could he?

He had felt like this child had stolen Jane from him. But Jane had made her own decisions.

Yes, his own failures were a part of that, but Jane had made her own choices. And on top of that, sometimes fate was simply cruel.

Mary had nearly died giving birth, and she had been innocent. Of anything.

The idea of Mary pale and bleeding made his blood run cold.

Even more so than the idea of her being round with child at such a tender age.

He needed to see her.

Holding the child still, he walked down the corridor, and to her chamber.

He knocked.

'Yes?'

He opened the door, and saw her lying in bed, her nightdress on, a hint of pleasured exhaustion present in the purple circles beneath her eyes.

The curtains were opened, allowing in a fair amount of grey morning air.

'Good morning,' she said. And then it was as if she suddenly realised he was holding the babe. 'Oh.'

'I thought about our conversation last night. I'm humbled by the story that you told of your clan leader. Would it be too painful for you if the child was named Lachlan?'

She looked stunned. Tears filled her eyes. 'Why would… How did my story bring you to this point?'

'Because you are why I'm standing here holding this child. I would've abandoned him. For what? I loved Jane. I don't even hate her in death. I had transferred all of my bad feelings to this little one, and he did nothing. Even my wife, with her share of guilt… I do not hate him. How can I hate him?'

He was his to protect. Just like Michael and Elizabeth. He was all this little boy had. He was all he had.

'That's beautiful. You are… You will be wonderful.'

'Only by comparison to the rest of my species.'

He came to sit on the end of her bed, and she looked scandalised, which he thought was rather charming.

'You have to leave before someone comes in.'

'I suppose I do.

'Come to me again tonight,' he said.

He thought that she would tell him no. That she would tell him they couldn't.

'I will. I will.'

And he knew then that it would be this way.

They could never be married. And he could never give her love. He did not know how. He was trying. Trying to shift these things inside of his soul so that he could get this child more of what he deserved. So that he could give his children something that they deserved.

But he would have her in his bed.

And that was still keeping things in their proper place.

She would be his mistress. But he also could not take her from the children, so she could not occupy that position publicly. She would be his mistress at night, and his governess by day. And that was how it would have to remain.

Chapter Seventeen

They settled into a routine of sorts, and if Mary allowed herself to simply live in each moment, then it was perfect.

He was a wonderful lover, and he taught her things about herself that she had never before known. Every night she went to his room, and she sneaked out in the morning before anyone could see. They had very much a distant, appropriate relationship by day. At night they made love, and lay in his bed naked, talking. Drinking, sometimes. One time he went to the kitchen and procured a tray of cold meats and cheeses. He had fed her grapes.

It was luxurious and wicked in a way that nothing in her life had ever been. More than that, there was no purpose to it. And she had a feeling that, for both of them, that was an entirely new sort of experience.

She had always been working towards something. Or running from something.

But she had never simply indulged in something for the sake of it.

She didn't think he had either.

Well, perhaps he had for short amounts of time.

'I am sorry if this is too personal,' she said, nearly laughing at saying something could be too personal when she was lying naked, his leg wedged between hers, her hand pressed to his bare chest.

'You can ask. I may not answer.'

He gave her a look of good humour…he had done that more and more lately.

He seemed content when they were together, and it was nothing short of a miracle. At least given what she knew of him. And she felt as if she knew him quite well.

'That is your prerogative. All right. How is it that Jane was not satisfied by you? My experience as your lover is that you are insatiable, and a woman would have to have an extra, secret number of hours in the day in order to take a paramour.'

He made a sound somewhere between a defeated growl and a groan, letting his head rest on the pillow. 'It is complicated.'

'I have the time for complicated.'

She had come to the conclusion these past weeks that she would rather miss sleep in favour of time with him.

'I do not wish for you to be offended,' he said.

'Why don't you test me, and see if it will offend me?'

He pulled her over onto him, so that she was lying across his chest, looking him in the eye. 'I cannot afford your offence, my darling. For what would I do without you in my bed?'

She pulled away from him, lying flat on her back. 'If that is the only reason that you wish to avoid my wrath, West, then I fear you may have offended me already.'

He rolled over so that he was above her. 'Do not say that, Mary.' He nuzzled her neck. 'You know that is not all I value you for. Also, I would not lie here talking to you long into the night when we should have slept hours ago.'

That made her feel warm too. Because it was the same for her. It was the same.

'I will not be offended. Or at least, I will not remove myself from you.'

She wouldn't. She didn't know how long this was going to last between them, and she would not miss a day of it.

She had thrown herself into this love affair with everything she had.

It was all-consuming.

It knit together confusingly with the work she did during the day. With the connection she now felt to his children.

To the bairn.

Lachlan.

They very much felt like hers in many ways, and it was painful. Painful to realise.

Because she had walked away from a child once. She hadn't been ready. And that child could not have been hers then.

But sometimes she felt as if this one could be. As if Elizabeth and Michael could be. She was a different woman now. She was a woman. Not a child.

She shoved those thoughts to the side.

'I told you my father was a horrendous libertine. He subjected all of us to his foul temper. And not only that, we all bore witness to the dissolution of his many love affairs. They were always tempestuous. There were suitors, men and women, who would come to our home in shambles after my father had made merry with their lives.'

'Oh,' she said.

'He cared nothing for the feelings of others. I am convinced he took both men and women as lovers not because he felt any genuine attraction to one sex over the other, but because there were different ways to play with their emotions, and he enjoyed that distinction. A man like him cares about only one thing, and that is himself.'

'And you bore witness to that.'

'Yes. When he was killed—shot, by the way, by a scorned lover—my mother's brother came to Attingham. He sat me down, and he told me that the one good thing my father ever did was spare my mother the disgrace, the indignity, of making her serve his more… His more creative desires. My uncle told me that a lady was gently bred, and you could not treat her the way that you did a prostitute at a brothel. I had some experience of prostitutes at that point. I was sixteen. My father gifted me a woman when I was fifteen.'

'West…' Horror stole over her.

'I know. It was yet one of the many things he did that crossed a line, one of the many things that was not appropriate in any fashion, and yet I did not know better at the time. Afterwards… Afterwards I felt no small measure of guilt. I did not go to a brothel again until some time later. I did not have intercourse with a woman again for several years. It was an experience that made me feel out of control. That made me feel shame. And I did not wish to repeat it. Not until I was in control. I did, however, by the time my uncle spoke to me have some idea of my… The flavour of my desires, shall we say.'

'I know no desires other than yours. Not truly.'

'I'm not a gentle lover,' he said.

She looked at the ceiling and smiled. 'No, you are not. I do not feel that a gentle lover would suit me. I like your strength. The way that you hold me. The way that you push me to the edge, but that I can trust you will hold me just there. That you will not let me fall.'

'I knew that I could not subject my wife to my appetites. That first night, when I licked you between your legs, it had been some years since I had done that for a woman. It was one of the things I could not ask of a lady. Our passion in the bedroom was tempered. By the fact that it was never fully what I desired.'

'I see.' She frowned. 'Why did you think that would offend me?'

'It is not gentlemanly to speak of one's past lovers to one's current lover, first of all. Also, I did not know how you would feel about…'

She rolled over onto her side. 'The idea that I'm not a lady?'

'I do not mean to cause any offence.'

'In truth, West, I am not a lady. And I understand that. Also… What you gave me is what I needed.'

'And it is what I need. I could not… I could never enter into something like what I had with Jane again. I failed her, I feel. We did not talk about this, not ever. We did not speak of what her desires might've been. She confessed, when she fell pregnant, that she had taken lovers many times over the course of our marriage. She needed a man who excited her more, and I could have been. I could've been, if I had not made a sweeping decision about how things would be conducted in our marriage, and by the time I realised where I had gone wrong it was too late to repair it. She was carrying another man's child, and at that point I could not… My pride did not allow me to lie with my wife while she was with child in that fashion.'

'Of course it didn't. You didn't fail her there.'

'I know. But I did fail her along the way. I did what I thought was right. I tried. I did the best that I knew to do. I did not want her to live out the same experience that my mother did. But she…' He stopped suddenly. 'She met the same end as my father. Killed, by extension, by her lover. I am doomed, it seems.'

She leaned in, and touched his face. 'You are not doomed.'

'It feels it.' He gripped her wrist and pulled her close, pressing their foreheads together. 'This is such a strange thing.'

'What is?'

'Speaking to you like this. I have never cut that deepest part of myself open and spoken words like this to another soul.'

'Neither have I. You were the only person to know the entire story of what happened to me in Scotland. And how I ended up here. I have kept that to myself. I have kept it and guarded it most fiercely, because I needed to become something and someone entirely different. I could not endure the shame of somebody knowing what had happened, but you took all the shame away from it. I did not hesitate to tell you, because when you came upon Pelham in the library, you believed me. You did not blame me. You have never blamed me and that is a rare thing. While I know it. My own mother blamed me. And my father would've killed me. After I had my son, I was kept in the castle until it was safe for me to travel. I never returned home.'

'Do you feel as if you left part of yourself behind?'

She shook her head. 'No. It is much more complicated than that. I feel as if I took all that I could with me, the broken pieces of that girl, and I fashioned something new. I have felt English for all these many years. I have felt like this was where I belonged. This life, this person. I made her into my truest self. She is me. But you have found a way for me to be honest about where I came from. With myself, and with you. To take all of it and stop hiding. At least with you.'

He nodded slowly. 'I will regret how unhappy my wife was for the rest of my life.'

'She could have also talked to you. Look at us. I took the measure of what sort of man you were from the moment we met. I know men. I told you that. I know when a man enjoys using his power to hurt others, because I have seen it up close. I know full well that what happened to me was an act of violence, because I could see the violence in that man's eyes. He wanted me to be small and reduced, and he wanted power over me. Like your father. A man who enjoyed the aftermath of the destruction, not the love. Not the affair. And I took the measure of you from the moment we met and I knew you were not that man. She could've seen it. You did not talk to her. But she did not speak to you. And you cannot bear all of the blame.'

He shook his head. 'That is where you're wrong. I am the Duke. And I set the intention for what we were. She would have feared voicing something that she thought I might not accept gracefully.'

'She thought you would accept her affair gracefully? Another man's child?'

'By that stage it was far too late. We built a wall out of small grievances. That is what occurs. Stone by stone, if you leave them there, they only grow higher. And tearing it down would have to be an intentional act, and when you are both steeped in your own dissatisfaction, you do not make such an effort. We were selfish. Both of us. I was angry she withheld her attentions, and as a husband I could have demanded them. I felt entitled, because I did not go to brothels. Because I did not get my pleasure elsewhere, and I had accepted less for our entire marriage than I truly desired. But of course I never enforced my husbandly rights. Because what I desire is not...'

'Submission does not come through force,' she whispered. 'You want surrender. That is entirely different.'

'Yes. As you said. That is what men like my father do, and in the end they are weak. In the end, the bullet wins. The consequences of the disaster that those men spend their life sowing. As happened to the man who attacked you, I believe.'

'Yes. Often in life, I feel there is not a surplus of justice. But in these instances…'

'Agreed. Jane was also angry at me. She found me cold and distant. She did not know how to connect with me. She wanted something I could not give, for our expectations of marriage were entirely different. Much like with the children. I thought that if I simply wasn't my father it would be enough.'

'Perhaps it is more important that you are you, West.'

'I don't know what that means.'

'This man, in bed with me. Naked. That man is the best that I have come to know. And the man that you are when we go on walks with the children. When you speak of your childhood.'

'I must write to my brother. I should have him and his wife and children visit.'

'Please do. Michael and Elizabeth would love that.'

'I have been distant from him. Primarily because of the babe. Because of Lachlan. I did not know how to explain the situation. Why he was not named.'

'Of course. But you should. Have him come. Have him come visit you and see you. He is your brother, and you…you are not your father, West. He should have a chance to see that you have made this home different.'

He nodded slowly. 'I will write to him.'

'Good.'

She saw the sky beginning to lighten outside and felt a stab of sadness. 'It is time for me to go. I feel that I cannot linger any longer.'

'I resent it,' he said.

She smiled. 'As do I.'

She dressed, and smiled at him one last time before she walked out of the door. And then, without thought, her face crumpled, and she had to stand there for a moment, holding back a wall of tears.

It was becoming harder and harder to walk away from him every morning. Harder and harder to keep those things separate. In the moment it was always glorious. Wonderful.

But after... After it was always pure sadness.

She would take the sadness for the joy that she felt when she was in his arms.

She was familiar with sadness. With loss and loneliness.

It was joy that she had never had before. And this was joy that surpassed all else.

She would take whatever pain earned her.

For the pleasure she had now.

Chapter Eighteen

Luke made arrangements to come and stay not two weeks later, and West felt anticipation at the idea of seeing his younger brother.

It was a strange thing to think that he would be able to sit with him, and not have to hold back quite so much.

Luke and his wife were so happy. Grace was a perfect match for him, and they seemed very much in love.

It was something that he and Jane had never exuded.

He thought of Jane's last accusation.

'It does not matter if you think you love someone, Samuel. You don't know how to show it. Your love is a desert, and a woman could die of thirst searching forever for an oasis.'

He had often thought, ever since, that his wife had died of thirst.

And then he realised something. He would still be lying to Luke. For he could not have Mary sit with them at dinner. She could not join him in the parlour afterwards for conversation. Mary was the governess. She was not his lover or his mistress in public.

He would not be able to acknowledge her, and that troubled him.

He put the thoughts of that aside when Luke, Grace and the children, Jacob, Marcus and John, arrived.

His sister-in-law moved in and gave him a warm hug. 'It is good to see you, West. We have missed you.'

'Quite so,' said Luke, grinning, but not hugging him. Instead, they shook hands.

'How was your journey?'

'Fine enough,' said Grace. 'Though the carriage ride made me a bit ill. As I am expecting another child.'

He felt a strange pain in his stomach at the revelation. 'Congratulations to you both.'

'Oh, please don't look like that, West,' she said, reaching out to touch his sleeve. 'I have had nothing but easy births. This will be no exception. You cannot be superstitious. I have my third child already, after all. This is the fourth.'

'Seems excessive,' he said to Luke, doing his best to regain his composure.

'I have been accused of being excessive, it's true.'

'I love him for it,' said Grace.

'You may send the children to the nursery,' he said. 'Michael and Elizabeth, and our governess are expecting you.'

'Quite good that you found yourself a governess, finally.'

He nodded. 'She is wonderful with the children. A revelation after those who were not able to draw them out.'

'You must be pleased.'

'I am,' he said.

They adjourned to the parlour and talked about London gossip, even though West didn't care. They couldn't speak only of business or Grace would be upset.

He checked the time and stood. 'It will be the hour that we have our time in the garden.'

'Your time in the garden?'

He nodded. 'I spend a couple of hours outside with the children every day. That is… Miss Smith's doing.'

It was a struggle not to call her Mary.

'Well,' said Luke, 'we ought to join you. I've not spent time in the garden at Attingham since I was a boy. And we did have great adventures.'

'We certainly did.'

When they went out to the sprawling lawn, the children were already racing around, five of them, and everyone screeching.

Mary was standing there holding Lachlan, looking out at the scene.

She was not required to care for him any more.

They had a wet nurse. Though he was near six months old, and was beginning to eat more food.

And Mary had taken on the care of him when he did not need to eat with ease.

It no longer seemed to hurt her. It seemed to be healing her.

In that moment, she looked down at the pudgy boy, her red hair blowing in the breeze, her green eyes bright in the beautiful sun.

And he did not think he had ever seen a more beautiful sight than this woman's love for a child she had not given birth to.

It made him feel fierce and protective of them both. For the child was not of his blood either. And it was beginning to feel... It was beginning to feel as if he could be. As if he were just one of the children. The same as the others.

It was a strange thought, transformative. His father could never have felt that, even for his own children.

Perhaps that meant something. Perhaps.

'Father,' Elizabeth yelled, bending down and picking up a fierce-looking wooden sword. 'You should be a pirate.'

'Excuse me,' he said to his brother. 'I've piracy to attend to.'

He broke away from his brother and his sister-in-law, and picked up his own sword, running after his daughter, who shrieked in delight.

And in that moment he could not recall having ever been happier.

Not even as a boy.

Not even then.

Suddenly, he was set upon by his son and his nephews, who took him out right at the knees and rolled him across the grass.

His brother laughed. The sort of laugh he had not heard from him since they were children.

And when they adjourned for dinner the only thing that dampened his happiness was that Mary could not join them.

She had taken dinner with the children and was now readying them for bed.

'I have to say,' said Luke as they were finishing, 'I have never seen you this happy. Not since we were children.'

'I am. I have… I found a new joy, I suppose, in the children.'

'I'm quite relieved to hear you say that, West,' his sister-in-law said. 'I worried. I worried you would resent the infant, and when you did not write to us to tell us his name…'

'Lachlan.'

'A strange name,' said Luke.

'Unconventional perhaps, but I named him after someone who was… Who is a great man.'

'Who?'

'You won't have heard of him. But he is the leader of one of the few remaining Highland clans in Scotland.'

'Very avant-garde of you,' said Grace. 'I like it.'

'Thank you.'

She laughed. 'I know you were not waiting for my approval.'

'No.'

'My brother is never waiting for anyone's approval,' said Luke. 'He is an island.'

Except he hadn't been. Not these past months. He had been with Mary. And all had been bright.

'The governess is lovely,' said Grace. 'Brilliant with the children, but she is beautiful. I cannot imagine that many wives would approve of their husband's hiring her.'

He felt an immediate kick of defensiveness on her behalf.

'She is very good at her work. And I resent the implication that she might be less able because of her beauty. Or perhaps that she might not be trustworthy.'

'I did not mean to imply she was not trustworthy, only that women are jealous,' said Grace. 'Many wives would worry such a pretty thing could take their place in their husband's bed. She is young. And striking.'

He could deny those things. But it was impossible. And he would only make himself sound the more guilty.

'That is true.'

He could feel his brother regarding him. And yet he said nothing. He would have to thank him for that later. Except if he did, it would expose them. And he did not care, not for himself, not now. Caring for the sake of propriety was something he just couldn't find in himself, not any more. But for her… For her sake, he would not expose this.

Unless…

Out here in the country… Did it matter? He was not married, could she be his mistress? He had a feeling his brother would not look down on her. Perhaps she could even take dinner with them. Grace, he could not be certain. It was entirely possible that his sister-in-law would not approve, and then would not allow the children to be around her. But…

He was not a married man. Many married men had mistresses living in houses adjacent to their wives. He could take dinner with her. She could sleep in his bed all night. And it would not matter what the servants said, for they were his servants.

No, she would not be able to go to London with him, she would not be able to participate in society, and he would have to get a new governess. It would only be right. But if he could have her…

He cleared his throat. 'She has made a world of difference to the children, and she could have the face of a Nordic troll, and I would still value her the same.'

Of course he would not have taken her to his bed, in all likelihood.

Or perhaps he would have. If she was still her. Still Mary.

'Whatever you've done with your life, do more of it,' said Luke. 'Because you are like a different man, West. I have never seen you so at ease.'

'Our father is dead,' said West.

Luke chuckled. 'Our father died twenty-four years ago. He has been dead a very long while.'

'Yes. But now I *realise* it. Perhaps it did take the death of Jane. Just to deeply understand how permanent the state is. Because I feel sometimes as if I've been waiting for him to return. And I had to stand as a pillar against everything he was just in case. But I'm not him.'

'No, West,' Luke said softly. 'You never were.'

'This place is difficult for you too.'

'Not so much now. But you had to live in it. When you were not in London. All these years, and it's been yours. I can well understand why it has felt burdensome to you. Why you have never quite felt free of him. He haunts this place.'

'Less and less by the hour.'

After dinner, Grace excused herself to go and tuck the children in, and Luke and West excused themselves to the parlour. West poured them both some brandy and had a seat.

'Tell me honestly,' Luke said, levelling his gaze at West. 'The governess. She is a damn sight too pretty to be a governess.'

'She is truly a governess,' he said.

'Nothing more? Only she looks at you as if the sun might rise and set on your every word. I watched you play with the children, but in part I watched her observe you.'

'Luke…'

'I am a married man,' he said, looking mock-shocked. '*Happily*. You don't need to worry about me, but if my older brother were having an assignation with an incredibly beautiful young woman I might like to *hear* about it.'

He could not lie to his brother, not about this.

'It is more than that.'

Luke cocked a brow. 'Are you in love with her?'

His denial was swift. 'Of course not. She's a governess, Luke. She is not a lady and she is not…'

Everything in him fought against that idea.

Love.

He had already killed one woman with his version of love.

'I understand the realities of the world, brother.' Luke looked amused. 'But you *are* screwing her.'

He clenched his jaw tight. 'Yes.'

'And to what end?'

He let out a breath, long and slow. 'I had the thought that I might make her my mistress. Openly.'

'A dangerous game to play with a woman's reputation. You would have to be prepared to *keep* her. And pay her a stipend for the remainder of her life, because she would never find work as a governess again.'

Luke was saying aloud what he already knew. If he made Mary his mistress, in truth she would be his responsibility for ever. But he did not hate the idea.

He could not imagine wanting another woman.

'I am prepared to do that.'

'A *deeper* commitment than marriage, some might say,' Luke continued as if he hadn't spoken. 'For if she has your children, they will be bastards. You will be consigning them to a life of relative disgrace, all because you could not let go of a woman you should never have touched in the first place.'

'I know that,' he said. 'You said that you wished to hear of my affair with a beautiful young woman, you did not say you wished to give me a lecture.'

'And you did not have to tell me of your plans to make her a mistress, or of your feelings. You could have left it at the physical, so I can only assume you wanted a lecture. What is it you are asking me? Because you *are* asking me something, Samuel.'

'What I am asking is if you would still come sit at my table. If my mistress sat beside me.'

Luke laughed. 'I was raised in the same house as

you. I don't care about propriety. All I care about is whether or not a person's actions are cruel. This has the potential to be, and I am reminding you of that.'

'I do not have a wife anymore.'

'I know. But your wife died only recently. And anyway, it is not that which concerns me. I wonder if you have thought fully about what it would mean for *her*. As you have pointed out, she is beneath you in status. The consequences for her will be grave.'

'She's smart. She will know what it means for her.'

He could see Luke sitting with that. Then he nodded slowly. 'You are right, of course. The lady will be very conscious of what it means for her. But does she believe her job will be in jeopardy if she refuses you?'

'No, she has freedom in this and she has been made aware of it.'

'You will have no judgement from me. Or Grace.'

'You're certain?'

He chuckled, looking down into his glass. 'My wife is an adventurous woman.'

'And what exactly does that mean?'

Luke lifted a brow. 'My wife and I have said vows to each other, separate to the vows one speaks in a church. Our own vows are unconventional. She and I enjoy a bit of pleasure-seeking. Often, we enjoy inviting another person into our bed. Grace is no prude.'

He stared in awe at his brother, whose wife was a lady, a gently bred one at that, who was a delightfully sweet wife and mother, and who was apparently an *adventuress*.

'And you are all right with sharing?' The very idea made him want to start a war. He would not share Mary with anyone.

'As long as I'm there to watch.'

'And you're not worried about her getting with child?'

Luke's brows lifted. 'I did not say they were men, West.'

'This might be a bit too intimate a conversation,' said West.

'You brought it up. I am only saying that Grace and I will have no difficulty sitting at your table. She will not judge a woman for her appetites. She has her own.'

'As long as we can be assured of your continued presence in the house.'

'Naturally. But you know that you could not take her to London. There will be whispers, of course. About your country mistress. But as long as your children have a proper governess I fail to see the issue. You're a duke. No one will judge you.'

'And as long as I keep her away from judgement you will not revile me.'

'Yes, indeed. And as long as you don't keep her once you take another wife.'

'I don't need another wife. I have enough money and enough children.'

'A very good thing. Then take her as a mistress, West, why not? There is no reason to deny yourself.'

'I have denied myself all of my life. It has seemed necessary.'

'You are not an indulgence away from becoming our father. Our father was such a hideous man. And his behaviour continues to be the stuff of legend. You are not him.'

'No indeed.'

And he realised he could've confided in his brother about Jane. But he didn't. Not because of Jane. Because of Lachlan.

Maybe some day. But not now. He wanted his brother to care for the child as he did Elizabeth and Michael. And he would protect the boy. Because, as his brother had pointed out, the true sin was if a person was wounded.

'Write to me. If you make that decision.'

'I will.'

'Do I have your permission to speak of it to Grace?'

He nodded slowly. 'It sounds to me, my dear younger brother, that you have a much more open relationship with your wife than I ever managed to have. And if I regret one thing about my years with Jane it's that I never did figure out how to speak to her. You and Grace have honesty. Cling to that. And tell her. Everything. Even if some of those things are my secrets.'

'A bit late to be receiving marital advice, but… You are correct. We have only ever been happier the more we share with one another.'

He would have to remember that. He would not share Mary, nor did he think she wished to be, but when it came to truth, he thought his brother had a point. He thought his brother was far more advanced than he when it came to the relationships in his life. West himself was only just learning.

But he would talk to Mary about her becoming his mistress.

The idea filled him with a sense of anticipation. He was set on his course now. And he would not be deterred.

Mary wished she had an easy way to procure new clothes but, living in the country as they did, it was difficult. What she had was the ruined chemise, torn partly down the centre, and a corset with very shallow cups for her breasts, which did not cover her nipples entirely.

The shadow of her intimate curls was visible through the diaphanous fabric. He might laugh. It was a silly combination of things.

But she thought that it had an edge of scandal to it that had the potential to light his blood on fire, and she thought his reaction would likely be incendiary. And she looked forward to it.

Concealing it under her dress meant pushing the edges of it down beneath the silk and revealing more of her breasts than she typically did, but she only made that change just before it was time to adjourn to his room. If she ran into Mrs Brown in the hall, the other woman probably wouldn't think overly much about it.

Thankfully, she did not, and she made her way carefully to his room.

He was there, standing at the end of his bed, half naked already, his glorious torso on full display. That broad chest, covered in dark hair, his flat, hard stomach tensing as she walked in.

'You started without me,' she said, noticing the evidence of his desire through his breeches.

'I've been thinking of you,' he said. 'It is difficult to keep my desire under control.'

'I do not wish you in control, West. I wish you to be wild.'

'I must ask you something.'

'Before you take me? I find that I'm impatient.'

She began to undo the laces at the back of her dress.

'Yes, before,' he said, his voice hard. She stopped. 'Continue,' he commanded.

So she did. Beginning to peel away the layers, to reveal the garment beneath.

His nostrils flared, his eyes going wide.

'What is that?'

'Remember my ruined chemise? I decided to make something useful of it.'

'You decided to make something that might well kill me.'

She laughed, feeling triumphant. 'My intent is not to kill you, darling, that would quite defeat the purpose.'

His lips curved, and she could not quite guess what he was thinking.

'What did you wish to speak about?'

'I have forgotten.'

'You haven't.'

He moved forward, growling and wrapping his arm around her waist, pulling her up against him. 'I would have your mouth on my cock now if I did not have something very important to say to you.'

'If my mouth is to be the one that's occupied, then perhaps you could tell me while I'm busy.'

Desire lanced her. Her heart pounding.

The need to put her mouth on him suddenly consumed her. She loved it when they did that. When he pushed his hardness between her lips and used her roughly. Thinking about it even now made her damp with need.

'Not yet,' he said. 'Mary…' He touched her face, his fingertips gentle. 'I have something to ask you.'

Whatever he asked, she would say yes. Whatever he asked, she would want it.

That was how it was with him. If she knew one thing, it was that.

'Anything you wish, Your Grace.'

'Remember when you told me you would not genuflect.'

'I do. Your Grace. My master.'

He growled. 'Stop. I need to be able to speak. Mary, I want you to be my mistress.'

She was taken aback for a moment, trying to make sense of what he had just said.

'Am I… Am I not your mistress, West?'

He frowned. 'Not in the sense that I am asking you to be. It would not be a secret. You would be paid an allowance.'

'I am paid to be the governess to the children.'

'It isn't the same as what I am asking. I am asking you to be my lover. You would be taken care of, and you would not be… You will not be accepted in polite society. But you would not be a servant either. When my brother came to visit, you would sit at the dinner table with me.'

'And what of the children?'

'They would accept you. They care about you a great deal.'

'But I would not be their governess.'

He shook his head. 'No. I would hire a different governess. Your job would be…'

'I would be a harlot,' she said.

He shook his head. 'No. It is not that. Many men have these arrangements. Many of them also have wives.'

'Will you take another wife?'

'No. Upon Jane's grave, Mary, I will not take another wife. It will be you. Only you.'

She would be his.

His. Not a member of the household staff, and not a governess. Not a lady, still. And not above reproach.

But she would be his.

She would not have to leave his bed, everyone in the household would know.

'You would move into a room next to mine.'

'Jane's room,' she said.

'Mary,' he said, 'I'm not trying to insult you with this offer. I want more. I was not satisfied welcoming my brother and his wife into the home and not being free to have you by my side.'

But they could not marry. He did not have to say that. A scandalous union it would be. A governess from nowhere. It would be better for him to have no wife, but she could not be his Duchess. His Duchess, of course not. What a foolish thing. A girl from Scotland who'd had a child at thirteen years of age could not be a duchess. She could be a governess, and she could be a mistress.

But she knew that. She did.

What was the purpose in being wounded by it? Why

would she accept nothing when she was never going to be allowed to have everything? She could have this.

And yet it did fill her with a sense of grief, because she did love the children. She did.

They were wonderful. She adored them. God in heaven, she did not wish to surrender their care to somebody else.

And she would not be their mother. Not really. And what would happen when her reputation was called into question by their friends…?

She knew that West was in a position where his taking of a mistress would not be extraordinary. It was only she who would experience the consequences.

She would be allowed into certain places that wives were not. If he went to a gentleman's club, she would likely be able to sit with him in certain contexts. A lover could be welcomed in places that ladies were not.

Just like a lover could be treated to rougher sex. Could be asked to get on her knees and put her mouth on his cock. She did not resent it, for she appreciated the honesty that existed between them. And yet. And yet it was just so difficult. To realise that she was ending up quite where she had hoped not to. But it was different now. It was. Because when she had thought of this fate before, the man hadn't been West. And now that it was West it was not simply a question of disgracing herself for a man.

It was about whether or not she wanted to solidify her connection to him. This was all he could offer.

And there was something tragic to it. But like all of her life. She had just thought this, only recently. She would rather have the joy that she had with him, and risk what came with it. She would rather have this than have respectability. Respectability she had never really had anyway. She had always been a pretender to this life. It had never been hers. But he could be.

And she could be his. And that was the deepest, most well-loved thing about his strength.

How much she wanted him to own her. Hold her.

There was tragedy in it. The children could never really be hers. But they weren't anyway. The moment they didn't need her she would be asked to leave, cut off as if she were nothing.

'If something were to happen between us,' he said, his voice rough. 'If something were to happen, you would be cared for, all the rest of your life.'

'Do you think that you will finish with me?' she asked, her voice small.

'No,' he said. 'I don't. I think that I will want you for all of my days. But I care too much for you to not make this plain.'

Yet again, his strength was in full effect.

Yet again, he was showing all the ways in which he was not like those other men.

He wasn't.

'Yes,' she said. 'I will be your mistress.'

She felt as if a layer had been stripped away from her. Her heart, possibly her soul, she felt joy, mixed with impossible pain.

This was the life a girl like her could have.

Truly, it was a life far beyond what she should have been able to aspire to.

This man was offering her an allowance for all of her life.

He was a duke. He would make sure she was cared for. And no, she would never be accepted in proper society, but she never would have been. Not ever. She was only a governess. She was a servant. And now she would be a disgraced woman, but the truth was she always had been. If anyone other than West had known the truth about her past, she would've been branded then.

They would not care if it were rape, she would be considered ruined. A woman who had given birth to a child.

This was elevated.

And she wanted him.

Could she not have what she wanted?

She wanted to wail. With joy, with deep, wrenching suffering.

He was what she wanted. She didn't care how she had him. She had been willing to take him like this, but oh, she could spend the night in his bed. She would be in the room connecting to him. He would buy her beautiful clothes. She would have servants.

Was there something wrong with her that she wanted that? That she wanted those things? She had struggled so much, and her mother had said she was a whore. So perhaps she would be. But a fine one. One that was safe and cared for. One that was with a man that she…

Oh, how she loved him.

And she wanted to be his.

She dropped slowly to her knees, stroking him through the dark fabric of his breeches. 'I will be your mistress,' she said. 'I'm yours.'

He grabbed her hair, angled her head back so that she was looking up into his face. 'Tell me.'

'I'm yours, Your Grace.'

'Yes, you are,' he said. 'Mine. No one else's. You will never belong to another man, do you understand?'

They were possessive words, but they were a promise to her. A promise of security, of safety and, most of all, of his loyalty.

It was brilliant. Bright and glorious inside of her.

'Show me,' he said. 'Show me your devotion.'

She undid the falls of his breeches with her now expert hands, and took out his gloriously familiar manhood, moving her hand along his thick shaft. She leaned forward, tasting him, before angling herself so that she could take as much of him as possible into her mouth. He was so big that it was near impossible to take him all, and she had discovered that she had a gift for pleasuring him this way. He had told her. Had told her that she was better than any woman he'd ever had. Perhaps it wasn't true. But she had a feeling that it was. Because West was, even when difficult, brutally honest with her.

Even in this.

He had never offered her pretty words. Had never spun her fantasies.

Never.

She hummed as she tasted him. As a flood of emotion rioted through her.

She was his.

She was his.

She showed him what that meant. How deeply she wanted it.

He held her hair, pulling and guiding her with his fists.

The pain was welcome, the pain kept her grounded.

Their play was always like this. Tinged with desperation, and an edge of something dark. But had their lives not been dark? Always.

He with his father, she with hers. They had always known, both of them, that life was not safe or easy or pretty.

But what they had together was brilliant and ugly all at once. Beautiful and hard enough to leave a bruise.

How she loved to be marked by him.

For she had been marked by so many other things in life.

She had been marked by giving birth to a child she had not wanted.

Oh, to be marked by him. She relished every chance she got.

She would be his, and it would be known. It would never be a mark of shame. Not to her. For she would not own the shame that the world tried to sell her. These things had been forced on her from the time she was a girl.

Shame. She did not feel it for what had happened to her then, and she would not feel it for choosing happiness now.

She would not. She took him in as deep as she could, and if that made her a whore, then so be it. For him, she would be.

She felt nothing but bliss.

He growled, wrenching her away from him, lifting her up, holding her hair and pulling hard as he brought her in for a savage kiss.

Something changed between them. This was no longer tenuous. This was no longer happening until perhaps it could not.

This was a commitment. Between the two of them.

They were taking ownership. Of what they did in the dark.

No longer content to pretend to be civilised creatures in public, while fierce and feral in private.

They were both of them marred by their truth.

Yes, he was a duke, and he would have substantially more protection than she. In fact, he would face no repercussion at all. But he would shield her. With all of his strength.

And as a woman in the world, that was truly all she could ask for.

'I need you,' he growled.

He drove her to the bed, turned her roughly and lifted her up with her back to him, positioning her on the bed on all fours. She looked over her shoulder and licked her lips in anticipation. He growled, placing his masculinity at the entrance of her body before he thrust in deep, holding her hips as he took her like an animal.

They were both animals in this moment. He was no better than her. They were equal here.

And in their lives, in this house, she knew they would be.

There would be barriers. But they would be worth it.

He filled her, over and over again, wrapped his hand around her throat and forced her chin upward as he held her fast, her back bowing as he took her, over and over again, his words incoherent. A growl. He made promises to her, both sweet and filthy, and she revelled in every single one.

Until she was full of it. Full of him.

Full of all of the emotion that she had for him.

So deep and raw and real.

And as her climax began to overtake her, as desire built up within her, so big and bright as to shatter her, she couldn't hold back any more. 'Samuel,' she said, broken, his name on her lips for the first time. 'Samuel, I love you.'

And on a growl he withdrew from her body and spent himself on the sheets. Always careful. So careful with her.

'I love you,' she said again.

But when he looked at her his gaze was bleak, and she knew that she had done something wrong.

But she wouldn't take it back.

She couldn't.

He said nothing, but she accepted that too.

He was a duke. And she was a girl from nowhere. Who could never be his governess.

She was in love with him. And he was a man who would never be able to love her back.

Chapter Nineteen

$$\mathcal{OSSO}$$

He woke up with her wrapped around him. And he knew well that he didn't deserve that.

He had offered her half. Less than. He had offered her a life of backdoors and secret passageways. Of whispers when she walked past. He had offered her these things as if his body was worthy compensation.

She loved him.

She loved him.

And he felt the wall inside of him quake.

He had loved Jane.

He had.

He had not in the end, and he knew that. Their love had been buried. Behind that wall of grievances they had built.

It had been crushed by it. Destroyed.

And what the years of distance and grievances had not destroyed, that act of betrayal had.

Still he had wept when she'd died.

The woman who had borne him children should

not have gone so soon. The woman he had bound his life to.

For he wondered how much of her vibrance had died because of him.

Because of what he could not give.

Because of his brand of love.

And he thought... What? He could spare Mary by not taking her as his wife? That it might somehow trick the devil within him, and make a situation where he could have this, and they could retain their glory without ever having to deal with the realities of life.

She loved him.

And that made all of those hopes and dreams he had been harbouring inside of himself arrive.

They were different, it was true. But was he different enough?

He did not know how to show love in this way.

He was only just learning to show the children, to be the father they needed, he could not...

He feared if he tried this too he would only fail and the stakes were far too high.

He had destroyed his wife.

It was the only way he knew how to be. For his father had been something else entirely. His father had let his emotions go unchecked, and yet they had destroyed all those that they'd touched, and how could he ever guarantee that his own feelings would not do the same?

Because what he felt when he saw Mary was violent. It was intense. Everything that he did to her in bed was a shadow of what existed inside of his soul when it came to her.

How could he be sure? How?

God in heaven.

A prayer as much as it was an epithet.

God in heaven.

He wanted her, he could not deny that, and now he had made promises to her. He could not send her away.

He did not see a scenario wherein he did not destroy her.

If he made her his mistress in public, as he had vowed he would do, as he had promised her he would, then he would kill her reputation in an instant.

If he kept her as his governess and they carried on in secret, it would kill her spirit.

If she loved him…if she loved him, regardless of what position she held in his life, she would be destroyed. And making her his Duchess would not fix that. It would not. For the truth was, he didn't care what society thought. She was well worthy of being his Duchess. She was more than worthy. That was the problem. What he had not wanted was for her to love him. What he had not wanted was for that to exist as part of the conversation. What he had not wanted was to destroy her. A wife of his could only end up a husk of who she had once been, and perhaps, perhaps he had believed that if she was his mistress the terms might be different. The expectations might remain something else. And yet.

She loved him.

And he wanted it. Everything within him, the walls, every last one of them, trembled beneath that certainty.

He knew what love was.

But he had never known how to show it.

For he feared it above all else.

And that fear had created so much destruction. If he could not avoid being his father by being his opposite, then…

You must be yourself.

Himself?

Easy to be when he was naked in his bed with Mary.

When he did not have to bear the responsibility of being a duke. When he did not have to also be a father.

He was undone.

She loved him.

He wrote to Luke, even though the letter would scarce arrive before he did, and he had his stablemaster ready his horse.

Mary came down the stairs as he was heading out the door.

'I must go to London,' he said. 'I will begin the search for a new governess there. I will be away some days.'

She looked stricken. He knew that she had not expected it, and of course it was not what she wanted to hear just the day after she had professed her love for him, the day after he had offered to change their arrangement. But he did help to reassure her by saying that he was going to enquire about a governess.

'If you must, Samuel.'

He wrapped his arm around her, aware that they had not explained things to the staff yet. Aware that somebody could walk in. 'I must. But it is all in hand.' He did not kiss her. He simply touched her face.

And he willed her to run away from him, he hoped that she could feel it. He would not betray the offer that he had made her, not now. It was too late. He had acted rashly.

Selfishly.

But he needed to speak to his brother, and he needed to do so immediately.

Luke was the spare.

He could do whatever he wanted, as evidenced by the fact that he and his lady wife clearly indulged in games that would have been made into rumour had it involved West.

'Then I will see you in a few days.'

'Yes. Look after the children. Send my apologies that I will miss our walks.'

'Of course.'

And then he left. And it felt as if a part of him shattered when he closed the door behind him.

Mary watched the children race about the garden and tried to smile at them. He had not withdrawn his offer to make her his mistress. They had slept together all night in his room and she had not moved back to her own room. His valet had seen them in bed together.

He had said nothing, of course. And Mary knew that afterwards Samuel would've spoken to him about it.

He had been attentive this morning before he had left, giving her a deep kiss before he had gone to his study.

She was still acting as governess until he replaced her, and she had gone quickly to her room to ready herself for the day.

But he was a different man when he had walked out of that house.

Something had changed within him.

He was... Distant. And hesitant.

She had said that she loved him, and she could sense that it was a mistake.

It was not a truth that he could manage.

What if he withdrew the offer?

She did not think he would. He was a man of honour. But did she stay in a position with a man who did not love her? With a man for whom her love created this... Conflict?

She looked out at the children again.

She could not leave. But she could offer to go back to being the governess. The very idea made her feel like she was being cleaved in two. She had lied to herself when she'd said she could take the sadness in trade for the happiness that she had experienced. For this was different. This was heartbreak.

It was not bearable.

It was too late anyway. The valet would've told everyone in the household that she had been in his bed this morning. They had begun that first, brazen move.

Mrs Brown would know.

They had not thought this through. They had been caught up in their desire.

What a strange thing to know that she could be.

What a brilliant and utterly wonderful thing.

She was as foolish as every woman. Everyone who fancied herself in love.

She was foolish, and so was he.

Then perhaps it was his cock and not his heart which had made the decisions here.

She could not be certain.

Either way, they had put themselves into a mess. One that could not be easily fixed. At teatime, she excused herself from the nursery and went to find Mrs Brown.

'Mrs Brown,' she said. 'I must speak to you...'

'Yes, girl?' The older woman fixed her with a stare.

'I assume that Cameron has spoken to you...'

She pursed her lips and Mary waited for her judgement. 'It was a topic of conversation in the kitchen this morning, if you mean your sleeping arrangements.'

'Yes.'

Mrs Brown sighed. 'I've known, Mary. It is not an easy thing to hide. And it is the way that the both of you are.'

'I'm sorry,' she said. 'I was not understanding of the wet nurse, and I helped in the loss of her job, and I am no better.'

'You still see to your work, Mary. You have never left the children on their own because of your relationship with the Duke.'

'Even so, I understand that I have compromised myself and my reputation...'

'You make him happy. The Duchess was a beautiful woman. And she could be lovely. She was fun with the children. When she had the time for them. But often she was occupied in her own mind. I knew she was having affairs long before the Duke did. But discretion is an important part of being a household manager. I would never have exposed her to his wrath. Though he is a kind man, a good man, nothing like his father. You make him happy. The way that you have taught him to be with the children makes him happy. That in turn makes the entire household happy.'

'I do not think I make him happy. He has gone off to London today, and I could see that he was bearing a great burden. I think he regrets asking... He has asked me to be his mistress.'

Mrs Brown looked at her, sadness and sympathy on her face. 'My darling, women have fallen for much less. You love him. It is clear to me he loves you.'

'He doesn't.'

'Even if he doesn't, to sacrifice for love is not a bad thing. I have never been in love. And no one has ever loved me. I would trade a life of propriety for the joy that he puts on your face. Yes, some might see it as disgraceful. But it is only because they're jealous.'

'I was at peace with my decision when I thought it would make him happy. But seeing the burden...'

'It's only because he knows he should offer you better.'

'He cannot. He cannot.'

'He is a duke. And he can do whatever he wants. And the sooner that he gets out from his father's shadow and recognises that, the happier you will all be.'

And then Mrs Brown left her to ponder those things.

It was not only Samuel who was under a shadow. She had been, all these years. And only with him had she begun to feel the sun shining upon her.

She had been brave, choosing this life. A life in England, away from everyone and everything she knew.

If Samuel wanted her, she would choose him.

This life. No matter how frightening it was. No matter how unknown. She had never come to England to choose society.

She had come because she'd chosen herself.

And she would choose herself now. Samuel, the children.

She could feel no shame in this. She loved him. She loved Lachlan and Elizabeth and Michael. How could she feel ashamed about love?

A life in the margins with him was better than a sterling reputation.

She could only hope he felt the same.

Chapter Twenty

'Come in. I'd only got your letter just an hour ago.'

He went into his brother's study, having been admitted to the townhouse by his butler a few moments ago.

'I need to ask you something.'

'Ask away.'

'How? How do you show love?'

'West. That is an odd question.'

'It is what I desperately need an answer to. Jane told me that my love was a desert. Jane… Jane hated me in the end, Luke. We were not happy. I loved her in the beginning. I wanted very much to be a good husband to her. To be a good father to our children, and I failed at it. Doing the only thing that I knew to do. Which was to be careful and controlled. I demolished all of that with Mary, and I still don't know. I don't know what to do.'

'West,' said Luke, moving to where he stood and clasping his arm. 'You must be willing to hurt for her. To be uncertain. You must be willing to say the wrong thing. To do the wrong thing. When you are hurt, you show her. When you are angry, you tell her. When you want something… You tell her.'

'We do well in bed. We have no trouble speaking there.'

'And the rest of it?'

'We speak of things. Of many things. She knows about Jane and I… I know much of her life. But I cannot help but fear that marriage to me…'

'Marriage? That is quite the upgrade from mistress.'

'If I am to do this, then I must do it, is that not so? If I am to be with her, then she must be my Duchess, is that not so? I cannot… I cannot bear it. I wish to present her to the world. I wish… I wish to God I lived a different life. So that it could be only about her. Only ever. I don't care what anyone else thinks, but they will be harsh. My governess, becoming my Duchess.'

'They will all know that you could've made her your mistress. And that she must be something quite extraordinary to be your wife.'

'Luke…'

'Just wait a year to get her in *that* way.'

'I have been careful there.'

'Good. Though accidents do still happen. My wife's condition being evidence of that. I had not especially wished for a fourth. Here we are.'

'I have been careful,' he said.

'It isn't important. You are a duke. You can do what you like.'

'I'm not concerned about that. My concern is that I will not make her happy. That I will trap yet another woman in my version of what love is. When I never saw it. And I wanted so badly to be a good husband for Jane, to be a good father.'

'Think. How have you changed things with the children? You live with them. You care about the things they care about. You run around with a wooden sword. Care about what she cares about. Do not presume to know what is best for her, ask her. I think that is your problem, West. You hoped that your feelings for Jane would be enough, that you could decide what was best based on that compass inside of you, but you did not consider hers. Already, I think this woman has shown you how to love her in ways that your wife certainly never did.'

It was true. Mary had told him all of her fears. And he had listened. But he had never truly asked her what she wanted. Because he had been afraid of the answer.

Afraid it would be something he could not give.

'I will stay here tonight if that is well. I must go back tomorrow.'

'Of course. Mend things with her.'

'And if I make her my wife?'

'I will be a bit disappointed that my starchy older brother did not in fact take a step into real scandal.

Honestly. To marry the beautiful younger governess…
You only make *me* look bad.'

'No one seems to care what you do. Why are there
no rumours?'

He laughed. 'Because if anyone knows what Grace
and I do in our spare time, it means they were present. And they cannot admit to that, now, can they?'

Society. So bound up by its own rules. It was not
enough to simply not be his father. To hold those rules
sacrosanct because his father had flouted them. Because he had surrendered all that power.

He had to decide what living meant for him.

And perhaps that was the lesson.

There was more to being good than simply not hurting others.

'Thank you, Luke.'

'You're very welcome. Life can be lived all kinds of
ways. Happiness takes many shapes. Grace and I are
happy. I understand not everyone would be. But we
are. Desperately so. Be happy. In your life that looks
like no one else's. Because it does not need to. Passion does not mean hurting others. Loving someone
does not mean you will cause them pain.'

He nodded slowly. And he realised there was no
way to be certain about any of this. Except he knew
he would do anything for her. As evidenced by the
fact that he was willing to cast aside all expectations
of him and marry her.

If she would have him.

He knew that what he had to do was stop making proclamations. And that would be the most difficult thing.

He would have to go to her a different man.

And he would have to figure out how to be that man between London and Attingham.

Because as for now, he had no answers.

Save but one.

He loved Mary Smith. And he loved Mary McLaren.

And he would do whatever he had to, to keep her love.

Days, he had said.

She felt bereft at not having him.

The suspense of not knowing what he would ask of her when he returned was unendurable. It was just after their walk, and the children had run ahead of her into the house where Mrs Brown had made them lemonade.

She was walking, her breast heavy as she moved, when she caught movement out of the corner of her eye.

And there he was. Walking across the grass, a shaft of golden sunlight casting him in an endless glow.

His white breeches fitted neatly to his body, his navy coat blowing in the breeze.

Everything in her stilled.

She wanted to run to him. And away from him.

But then, his pace quickened. And he was the one running. To her.

He reached her, and cupped her chin, tilting her face up to look at him. And then he did something utterly unexpected.

The Duke dropped to his knees before her and wrapped his arms around her.

'Mary,' he whispered.

She put her hand on the back of his head and held him like that. Held him there against her.

'Mary,' he whispered again fiercely.

'Samuel.' She moved her fingers through his hair, stroked his face.

'I had to go and see Luke. I am sorry. I did not hire a governess.' He looked up at her, and judging by the sorrow in his eyes, she was afraid she knew what might come next. That he would ask her to remain a governess.

And she realised she would do it for him. For the children.

She had purposed not to take half. But a life without him at all, his friendship, his warmth…it was less than half.

A life without the children she had come to love was empty.

She would miss being his lover.

But she would miss him altogether if she left him.

She had been alone, for years. And even before she'd gone to his bed, she'd found something here.

Something that made her feel part of this family. She would cling to it.

'I love you,' she heard herself say. 'And I will do so in whatever way you need me to.'

'What do you mean?'

'If you cannot make me your mistress, if for the children you need me to stay I...'

'Mary,' he said again, her name a fierce prayer on his lips. And then he stood and pulled her to him. 'I am done issuing edicts. I thought that love was to create safety and certainty, and the only way I knew how to do that was to make all of the decisions. To hold myself separate. I loved Jane. But I did not know how to show it. I loved her, but I allowed it to be an unequal love. It was not about her, but about what I thought her to be. Because I did not listen to her, and I did not ask what she wanted. Someone told me what a lady wife wanted, and that is what I did. I never asked what my lady wife wanted. I never saw love. I did not know how to show it. I am trying...'

His voice broke. This duke. This strong, powerful man. This man who had taken her into his arms and shown her what good could come from a man's strong hands.

This man who knew all the ways to pleasure her body.

This man who had been stoic when telling her about his wife's death. About the child that wasn't his.

This man broke looking at her.

'Mary, I love you. All that you are. The things that you have shown me and told me. And I tried yet again to make a decision for you. I asked you to be my mistress. But I did not ask you what you wanted. What your dream is for this life.'

'Do not ask me that. Please do not ask me that, because it is cruel,' she said, her heart beating fast.

'Trust me,' he said, holding her chin. 'You have trusted me with your body. You trust me to hold you in the most vulnerable of ways. Trust me that I will not play dangerous games with your emotions. I will not.'

'Do not make me say it without telling me what you are willing to give.' He had said he would not marry. He had said he would not on his wife's grave and now she could not think how or why it would have changed.

'I would make you my Duchess.'

She shook her head. 'You cannot.'

He all but growled. 'I am a *duke*. And what is the point of it if I cannot do what I wish? I will make you my wife. And what difference will it make? If you are my mistress they will whisper behind their hands. If you are my wife they will not dare.'

'*Why?*'

'Because I don't want a fraction of it, I want it all.'

'You said you would not marry.'

'I did not want you to love me. I did not want to risk loving you. But it is too late. Because I do not want you to be my children's governess, a woman in the shadows, I want you to be their mother. Because you have done more for them in this short time than I certainly ever managed to do. You love them. As you love me. In more ways than I deserve, that is certain. And I had the audacity to think of you as a woman from nowhere, with uncertain parentage. My father was no better than yours, they simply gave him a title to go along with his bad blood. Life has made so many decisions for us, but we can make this one. If you do not wish to be my Duchess, then be my mistress. If you do not wish to be my mistress, to be my governess. Only do not leave me. Please. I will not make the decision for you. You must choose what will make you happy. I nearly chose not to tell you that I love you because I wished to protect you from the very thing that I felt destroyed Jane. But it was not my love. It was all the things I held back. And I will hold nothing back from you. You have my word.'

She broke then, flinging herself into his arms. 'Samuel.' She kissed him, hard and firm. 'I will be your Duchess. Because I want everything. If that makes me selfish, then I suppose that I am.'

'No more than I am,' he said. 'Because I do not deserve you. Your love, your patience. Your passion.'

She felt awed by him. Broken open by his words. 'Do you have any idea…? You are the first person in all the world to make me feel as if I am not a consolation. You make me feel right, Samuel. Unafraid. Loved. You have banished my shame.'

'And you have shown me how to feel. Really and truly. You've shown me how to better make myself into more than simply a man with a good reputation. But a man who is truly good. To those around him. The ones that matter most. My wife. My children.'

She closed her eyes, happiness echoing through her.

My wife.

Mine.

She had never belonged to anyone. And she would belong to him.

'One can never be prepared for a duke,' she said, touching his face.

'I don't understand.'

'It is what I thought when I first saw you. But I really did not know. I could never have prepared for how you would change my life. I never believed that love would be for me. I never believed that I would truly have a home. All I wanted was stability. All I wanted was to survive. But you have given me...'

'Look at all that you have given me. To not make the mistake of thinking that I have been overly generous with you. I would've stayed locked in that study for the rest of my life. I would never have known my children. I would never have picked up a wooden sword again. Lachlan would never have been my son. You showed me how to love in a way that reached beyond boundaries. And that was what we all needed.

'My Duchess,' he said.

'Your Grace.'

'I rather hope that with your elevated title you will still genuflect.'

'When naked, Your Grace.'

'I love you.'

And she knew that she would never tire of hearing it. Not ever. For all her days. And she knew also that she would hear it every day for ever.

She had been looking for stability. But she had got so much more.

She had got a family.

She had got love.

Her canvas had been painted impossibly bright. Because she was never ruined. She was loved.

Epilogue

They had known that he was coming.

There had been letters exchanged between Lachlan and Samuel, Penny and Mary. They had known that he was coming. But of course that did not mean they felt prepared.

One thing about the way that they had chosen to conduct their lives these last ten years was that they had been honest, always. Their honesty with Elizabeth had caused some trouble, particularly when Elizabeth had explained procreation to her friends during her first season.

Elizabeth felt that every woman should be prepared. She felt this strongly, because her mother felt that strongly.

They did call Mary Mother eventually.

Mary had been very conflicted about it, because even though she had held some ill will towards Jane for the difficulties that the two of them had had, she respected the love the children had for her.

Elizabeth had assured her that she could think easily of both women as her mother. And that it was not about forgetting Jane, but loving Mary.

Lachlan, of course, knew no other mother.

And he was theirs. As surely and certainly as Elizabeth and Michael. And Victoria, Florence and Daniel. The three that had come quickly after Lachlan. At least they had been married six months before she had got with child. There had been no opportunity for the ton to start rumours that they'd been obligated to marry.

But of course he was a duke, and he was obligated to marry no one. And Mary was so lovely and delightful that in the end they could never freeze her out entirely.

She had actually become a rather scandalous darling in society. And now the half-brother they had been told of but had never met was coming.

After Mary and Samuel had wed, she'd finally written to Lachlan and Penny to ask after her son. To say she wanted to be kept informed of his life. She'd discovered that they had raised their son with the knowledge that he had been born of a woman that he didn't call Mother.

Mary had always thought it best to keep her distance when he was a child. Samuel had offered to take her to Scotland. And Penny and Lachlan had been open to that as well.

But she had felt it best to give them space and time. And that if he wished to ever see her, he would be welcome. And it so happened that he was coming to London for the first time. And had decided that he did in fact wish to meet the woman who had given birth to him.

When the door opened, Mary bypassed Barrows. And stopped, putting her hand over her mouth. West had to fight the urge to rush forward. Because he knew that he needed to give his wife a moment. And then a very tall young man with red hair came over the threshold. And Mary went straight into his arms.

And West knew he did not have to keep his emotions back. He didn't any more.

Because Mary had shown him a better way.

He could never have prepared for Mary.

And thank God.

Thank God.

She parted from her son and held onto his face. 'It is very good to see you,' she said.

'It's good to see you too.' He grinned at her then. 'I have quite a lot to tell you.'

'I can't wait to listen.'

* * * * *

COMING SOON!

We really hope you enjoyed reading this
book. If you're looking for more romance
be sure to head to the shops when
new books are available on

Thursday 20th
July

To see which titles are coming soon, please visit
millsandboon.co.uk/nextmonth

MILLS & BOON®

Coming next month

A LAIRD WITHOUT A PAST
Jeanine Englert

Where are my clothes? Why am I naked?

What was going on?

A dog barked, and Royce lowered into a battle stance putting out his hands to defend his body.

'Easy, boy. Easy,' he commanded.

The dog barked again and nudged his wet nose to Royce's hand. Royce opened his palm, and the dog slathered his hand with its tongue and released a playful yip. Royce exhaled, his shoulders relaxing. He pet the dog's wiry hair and took a halting breath as his heart tried to regain a normal rhythm.

A latch clanked behind him followed by the slow, creaky opening of a door, and Royce whirled around to defend himself, blinking rapidly to clear his vision but still seeing nothing.

'Who are you?' he ordered, his voice stern and commanding as he felt about for a weapon, any weapon. His hand closed around what felt like a vase, and he held it high in the air. 'And how dare you keep me prisoner here. Release me!'

'Sailor's fortune' a woman cried. 'I think my soul left my body; you gave me such a fright. You are no prisoner,' a woman stated plainly. 'By all that's holy, cover yourself. And put down the vase. It was one of my mother's favourites.'

Light footfalls sounded away from him, but Royce stood poised to strike. He stared out into the darkness confused. Where was he and what was happening? And why was some woman speaking to him as if she knew him.

The door squeaked as it closed followed by the dropping of a latch.

'Then why am I here?' he demanded, still gripping the vase, unwilling to set it aside for clothes. Staying alive trumped any sense of propriety. She might not be alone.

'I cannot say. You were face down in the sand being stripped of your worldly possessions when I discovered you.' A pot clanged on what sounded to be a stove. 'Care to put on some trews? They are dry now.'

'Are you alone?' he asked, shifting from one foot to another staring out into the black abyss.

'Aye,' she chuckled.

He relaxed his hold on the vase, felt for the mattress, and sat down fighting off the light-headedness that made him feel weak in the knees.

'Could I trouble you to light a candle if you do not plan to kill me? I cannot see a blasted thing, and I would very much like to put on those trews you mentioned.'

Continue reading
A LAIRD WITHOUT A PAST
Jeanine Englert

Available next month
www.millsandboon.co.uk

LET'S TALK

Romance

For exclusive extracts, competitions and special offers, find us online:

- **f** MillsandBoon
- **t** @MillsandBoon
- **O** @MillsandBoonUK
- **d** @MillsandBoonUK

Get in touch on 01413 063 232